AMBER FISHER

SIN &
BEAR IT

LIGHTS, CAMERA, MYSTERY

I

one

. . .

I knew something was wrong the minute I walked into our apartment.

The bookshelves were ransacked, with books lying scattershot all over the floor around them. The couch was pushed away from the wall where it belonged, and the knick-knacks over the fireplace were missing. Clothing was strewn helter-skelter across the living room floor, and our potted plants had been moved from their proper places and were now lined up against one wall.

My throat tightened. My stomach flipped. I stood still as stone, hardly daring to breathe, my senses on high alert as adrenaline coursed through my veins.

We were being robbed.

But just as I was deciding what to do—call the cops or grab a baseball bat? Did we even have a baseball bat? —I noticed something aside from the disarray.

The astringent scent of cleaning products.

I started moving toward the bedroom. I was halfway through the living room before I noticed the suitcases lying open on the couch, half packed. I peered inside, my brow wrinkled. Shayda's blouses, t-shirts, and sweaters were neatly folded, not haphazardly thrown inside. I pawed around the garments, looking for my things, but everything in the suitcases belonged to Shayda alone.

What was happening? Why were our suitcases packed with Shayda's things in the living room? Why was our apartment in such disarray?

I smoothed the garments back into place and took another look around. On second look, it no longer appeared to be a robbery. What few valuables we had, like our PlayStation and my laptop, were still where they belonged. Plus, there was the smell. Thieves didn't usually wipe down the counters with bleach, not even if they were worried about fingerprints. So it probably wasn't burglars, but still, something was off.

I was headed toward the bedroom when I nearly collided with Shayda in the hallway. Her hair was tied away from her face with a bandana, and she wore a pair of pink rubber gloves. She stopped in her tracks, her eyes flying wide as she clutched her chest and yelped with surprise. When she realized it was me, I expected her face to flood with relief.

It didn't.

She stood still, her jaw clenched and nostrils flaring. Then, she dropped her arms to her sides and blew out a heavy breath. "I wasn't expecting you back yet," she said.

I glanced at my smartwatch. It was noon, which

seemed a normal time for me to come home for lunch. "What time were you expecting me back?" I asked.

Shayda gave a lame shrug, her expression unchanged. "I don't know. I never know *anything* with you these days."

I stood still, thinking of what to say as I shuffled through the encyclopedia of Shayda's facial expressions stored in my brain. My therapist said I was getting better at recognizing emotions, especially Shayda's. We lived together, so I had a lot of practice. I still wasn't great at it, though, and I usually tried to mask my lack of emotional intelligence by talking. But that didn't work with Shayda, so as she stood there glowering at me, I kept my mouth shut.

Finally, her expression registered.

Exasperation. A lot of it.

"You're upset that I didn't come home this weekend," I said. "I know. It's just that there was a new break in the case, and you know how I get when I'm deep in my work. So I just thought—"

Shayda held up a hand to interrupt my explanation. "I don't care, Sid. Save it. All the explaining, all the excuses, none of it matters anymore. I gave this a good college try, but I think we're just..." She sighed, squeezing her eyes shut. "I think we're just done here."

I paused, letting her words sink in. "What do you mean, done here?"

Shayda sighed, shifting her weight to one leg as she crossed her arms over her chest. "What day is it today, Sid?"

I shrugged, hoping this wasn't a trick question. "Monday?"

Shayda's eyes narrowed. "Right. And what's the date?"

Again, I shrugged. Now I was pretty sure these were trick questions. "May 31st?"

Shayda tapped her fingers against her elbows, her posture rigid. "So if today is Monday, May 31st, then yesterday was what?"

"Yesterday was Sunday. May…"

I let my voice trail off. My stomach sank as I finally realized why Shayda was upset. It wasn't because I'd stayed gone all weekend without telling her. "Oh, no," I groaned, my voice low and full of remorse. "Shayda. Yesterday was your sister's wedding."

"That's right!" Shayda shouldered past me, marching into the living room and snapping off the gloves, which she tossed to the floor. "My baby sister's wedding. My *entire* family was in town, including my grandparents, aunts, uncles, and cousins who flew in from Iran—that's halfway across the world, Sid. But *you* missed it. You promised you would use this opportunity to finally meet my family. We've been together for three years, Sid, and my family's never met you, not even once. You were supposed to be there."

I raised my hands to my face and dug my knuckles into my eyes. "I know. But with everything happening at work, I just forgot."

That was apparently the wrong thing to say. Color shot into Shayda's cheeks, and the muscles in her jaw clenched. Tendons stood out like ropes along her neck. I didn't need my mental encyclopedia for this one. Shayda was furious. "You forgot. Do you know how that sounds? How do you forget something this important? You were supposed to put it on your calendar. You were supposed to set a reminder. I called you, Sid. But do you know where your phone was?"

I took a deep breath. "Here?"

"You got it," she said, her words underlined by a dry, unamused chuckle. She pulled my phone from her hip pocket and tossed it to me. "You forgot the wedding, and I couldn't even get in touch with you to find out what happened. We *talked* about this. We agreed there couldn't be any mistakes this time. And God, I just meant I didn't want you to say anything inappropriate to my family. I didn't think I had to explain that you had to actually *be* there!"

As usual, I didn't know what to say. My mouth was dry, and I tried to swallow around the lump in my throat, but I couldn't. I was desperately thirsty all of a sudden, and I wanted to go into the kitchen for a glass of water. Not only would that give me time to think, but it would get me out from under Shayda's accusing glare. Not that I didn't deserve it. I did. And if I were a normal person, I'd sweep her into my arms and apologize profusely, promising it would never happen again.

But that would be a lie. It probably *would* happen again. And worse, I couldn't apologize. The words "I'm sorry" always stuck in my throat like glue, refusing to budge. It's one of my worst flaws. I can't apologize. Ever. I'm too proud.

Or stubborn. Or idiotic. Something.

I gestured toward the luggage. "So, where are you going?"

She stared at me, mouth agape, momentarily at a loss for words. Then she blurted out, "Are you *serious* right now?"

I blinked. "Of course I am. You know I don't joke about stuff like that."

Shayda pinched the bridge of her nose and closed her eyes. When she opened them again, they were damp, and her face had gone slack. "Sid, I'm moving out."

I stared at her for a moment, too surprised to speak. I watched her fidget, knowing she was waiting for a response, but my mind was blank. So I said, "What do you mean, moving out? Hold on, Shayda. Hold on." I ran my hands through my hair, buying myself some time. I should have gone for that glass of water. "You're upset. I see that now. And I know I screwed up. I know I screwed up *bad*. But moving out? Isn't that a little…extreme?"

Shayda's shoulders slumped, and she pressed her fingers to her eyes, her cheeks ruddy. "It would be extreme if this were the first and only problem between us. But things haven't been great for a long time. I'm sick of cooking dinner for two, only to eat alone. I'm tired of you not coming home but also forgetting to call. I'm done wondering if you and I are really on the same page about this relationship. I'm so tired of you not understanding how I feel. I really wanted to make this work. I tried and tried and tried. But now I just want this to be over."

She dropped down onto the couch, trembling. Her skin had gone pale, and her eyes were glassy. She was about to cry. I held my breath, debating what to do. I knew I should go to her, say the right words, and caress her skin. I was supposed to comfort her, but I didn't want to. Not because I wanted her to be upset, but because comforting people made me feel like a phony. On the other hand, my therapist said sometimes I have to do things for Shayda I don't want to do because that's what being in a relationship is about. But, if what Shayda said was true, then I wasn't in a relationship anymore, and I didn't have to comfort her if I didn't want to.

I stood there like an idiot, debating what to do for too long. While I argued with myself over the pros and cons of comforting my girlfriend (?), Shayda covered her face with her hands and began to sob.

Teary eyes, I could ignore. Sobbing was a whole different story. I sat beside her, awkwardly draping an arm around her shoulder and pulling her close to me. She didn't resist. I let her cry for a while until she finally pulled away and wiped her eyes dry. "I really do want the best for you," she said, her voice wet and sniffly. I wanted to get up to get her a tissue, but I didn't think that was the right thing to do, so I stayed where I was. "But I do think it's gonna be hard for you to find someone who can put up with everything. Your crazy schedule, your weird job, and all the other…stuff."

"Stuff?" I repeated. "What stuff?"

"Sid." Shayda gave me a look. "You know what I'm talking about."

Oh. She was talking about the ghosts.

I'm a ghost whisperer. I can see, hear, and interact with ghosts, and I've been doing it since I was a kid. It was a long time before I realized that not everyone could see spirits. It was an even longer time before I realized it freaked people out when I talked about them. In general, people either thought I was crazy or a creepazoid, neither of which was true, and neither of which I wanted anyone to believe. I already had enough working against me, being maladroit at interpersonal interactions and having little ability to read situations, especially emotional ones.

That's one of many reasons I loved Shayda. She didn't mind that I saw the ghosts. Well, she minded, but it didn't creep her out, and she didn't think I was nuts. Of course, I didn't tell her about all the ghosts I saw. Especially the ones I knew she wouldn't want to hear about, like the ghosts of people that jumped in front of trains or fell off bridges or especially the ones that got stabbed or shot to death. I saw those people frequently, thanks to my job. The ghosts looked exactly as they did in death: broken and bleeding and half put together. It didn't bother me, but Shayda didn't like to hear about those things. After all, she was a "normal person." Not psychic. Not weird.

"I promise I'll try harder," I said. I tried to reach for Shayda's hand, but she pulled away, climbing to her feet. "I can get better. At everything. Really, I can."

"That's the thing, though," she said, shaking her head as the corner of her mouth dipped into a little frown. "I don't think you can. Not on your own."

I held my hands out. "I'm not doing it on my own. I have a therapist."

Shayda sighed. "When was the last time you saw Dr. Xena, Sid? Like, when was the last time you *actually* kept an appointment?"

I opened my mouth to object, then snapped it shut. She was right; I technically had a therapist, but I mostly dodged her calls and avoided seeing her. The thing was, I was pretty sure Dr. Xena had already done everything she could for me. I didn't like leaning on other people. I didn't like asking for help and seeing Dr. Xena made me feel weak. I'd learned enough to make things work with Shayda, and that had been good enough for me.

Except, now I didn't have Shayda. So I didn't know where that left me.

"I know you have a hard life," Shayda was saying. Her eyes had gone soft and wet again, but I didn't think she would cry this time. "Your personality quirks aren't that big a deal. You can manage them—you just need to *ask* people what they're feeling or what they mean if you don't know. You can manage that part of it, Sid. But the stuff with the ghosts? Your job? I don't know if you can handle all that on your own. It's a *lot*. You know? And on top of your psychological stuff…"

"There's nothing wrong with my brain," I interrupted. "My brain is *fine.*"

"I never said it wasn't," Shayda shot back. "Your brain is *more* than fine. You're brilliant and funny and kind. But forgetting a wedding? Not coming home for an entire weekend and not calling me? Those aren't things…"

I knew she was going to say, *"Those aren't things normal people do,"* and I was glad she didn't because that would have pissed me off, and I didn't want to be angry on top of being hurt and scared. Instead, she said, "Those aren't things I can deal with." She was using a technique she tried to get me to use: she made her words about herself rather than about me.

But I knew they were really about me.

"Please get help, Sid. Talk to someone. Everybody needs help sometimes. It's nothing to feel bad about."

I looked down into my lap. "I don't need help," I said. "I've got everything under control."

Shayda sighed. "That pride is going to be the death of you. You know that, right?"

I said, "I don't want to talk about this, Shayda. Can we please not talk about this?"

"Fine." The woman who used to be my girlfriend zipped up her suitcases and carried them to the door. "Either way, this is over between us. Okay? We're done. I'm sorry."

We didn't speak more after that. I didn't know what else to say, and I wasn't going to beg her to stay. Besides, I may not be good at reading people, but even I knew Shayda wasn't going to change her mind. But I didn't want to hang around and watch her pack up, either. So as she loaded up her car with plants and art and suitcases, I went for a long walk to clear my head and cry where no one would see me.

When I came back, Shayda was gone.

And then my phone rang.

two

. . .

"Is this Sidney Sheridan?"

I winced as I sat down on the sofa, now devoid of suitcases. No one called me Sidney. "This is Sid," I said.

"Hi, Sid. My name is Tricia Woodward. I'm a producer at RealTV Productions. Do you have a minute to chat with me?"

I leaned back into the cushions, closing my eyes. I got calls like these every now and then—reality TV producers who wanted me to appear on some stupid show about paranormal investigators, ghost hunters, things like that. Most of those people were actors. Phonies. I hated people like that. They made me look bad, and I didn't need any help in that department. "Now isn't really a good time," I said.

"I understand. I won't be a moment. I'd actually like to schedule an in-person meeting with you to discuss a new opportunity we think you'd be perfect for. Do you have any time this evening? I'm in town," she explained.

"Yes," I said, instantly regretting it. I naturally default to the truth, often to my detriment. "I mean, I have time this evening, but——"

"I'd be happy to meet you anywhere convenient for you. Is dinner or coffee preferable?"

I sighed. Shayda did most of the cooking, and I didn't have any idea what was in the refrigerator. "Dinner, I guess," I said. I was heartbroken, but I still had to eat.

"Wonderful! I'll text you the address. How does 8 o'clock sound?"

"That sounds fine," I agreed, my voice sounding weary even to my own ears. "Sounds great."

"Wonderful. See you then."

The line went dead.

———

The address Tricia Woodward sent me was for a fancy French restaurant on the other side of town. That was a bad sign. Bad because it meant the production company was pulling out all the stops to get me on board with whatever cockamamie project they'd cooked up in some ridiculous board room. I didn't like being pressured—I guess no one does—and even walking into the restaurant set me ill at ease. I'd almost made up my mind to turn right around and leave when I saw her.

Seated in the waiting area dressed in a simple linen dress, Tricia Woodward wasn't anything I expected. Usually, when the production companies came after me, they sent some artificial-looking person who spent too much time in front of a mirror. You know the kind. Perfectly coiffed hair, glowing white teeth, fake charisma oozing from their pores. I guess that works with some people. Not with me. Beautiful people made me self-conscious. I was nothing special: average height and build with a never-before-coiffed head of short, chocolate-brown hair. My eyes were my best feature, but they were just brown. I say they were my best feature because that's what I was told, but maybe everyone who said that was just being polite because otherwise, there was little to compliment me on.

I'm not being pitiful. That's just the truth.

But anyway, Tricia wasn't anything like that. She had dishwater blonde hair and fine lines around her eyes; not the kind that made her look old but the kind that made her look friendly. She was even wearing white Keds, which I didn't think they made anymore. She looked normal. In fact, she looked so ordinary that she reminded me of Shayda, which got me feeling all emotional again. But I swallowed it down and donned a fake smile. But not too much of a smile. I didn't want Tricia to get the wrong idea.

She rose to her feet, extending a hand which I accepted. "Thanks for agreeing to meet on such short notice," she said. "This isn't how I like to do business. But the opportunity came up, and since I was in town, I figured I would see if you were available. Looks like I had pretty good timing."

I didn't bother to tell her that her timing was actually garbage, that my girlfriend had just broken up with me, and the last thing I wanted was dinner with a shyster encouraging me to shove my ethics in a corner and do a show I didn't believe in. But I had been right about the refrigerator at the apartment: it was mostly empty. And like I said before: I had to eat.

The hostess sat us at a table in the far corner of the main dining room. After I placed my napkin in my lap, I folded my arms over my chest. "So, what's this all about?"

Tricia smiled. "You like to get right to the point, don't you? Suits me just fine. Okay. We have an idea for a new reality TV show. Now before you say anything, hear me out," she said, holding up a hand to stave off my objection. "I did my research on you. I know our network and several others have made similar offers in the past. And I understand why you were hesitant to accept those offers. Most of the shows they pitched were…" She dithered, tilting her head side to side, equivocating. "Let's just say, maybe not entirely on the level. But this new TV show is different from the others. There are no haunted locations to investigate, nor are we pitching a half-baked 'Where's Bigfoot?' adaptation. This is something entirely new." She clasped her hands on the table and leaned forward. "Have you ever seen the Japanese TV show Paris House?"

I shook my head. "No. What is it?"

"The show takes six young people and puts them in a house together. Six strangers. Most of the people coming to the show hope to find love, but others have different objectives. There's no script or interviews or anything phony like that. The participants merely live in the house together, and the crew films their lives. Simple."

It sounded simple. It also sounded like nothing I would ever watch, let alone participate in. "Okay. So, what does that have to do with me?"

Again, Tricia smiled. "I'm glad you asked. The idea for our TV show is a little different from the Japanese version. We want to take a number of strangers—seven, however, not six—and put them in a house together in sunny Odyssey, California, a beach town not too far from here. But we're not interested in just *any* strangers." Her smile deepened, and I thought I saw a twinkle in her eye. "What would happen if you took seven strangers, each guilty of one of the seven deadly sins, and put them in a house together? Would they get along? Would they learn from each other? And more importantly, would viewers learn anything from watching them?" Tricia lifted her hands, palms out, making little exploding motions with her fingers. "Seven strangers. One common theme. *Sinful House*: Which sin is your favorite?"

She was looking at me expectantly, her eyes wide and glittering, that smile growing by the second. But I had no idea what she wanted me to say. Nothing made any more sense now than when she started talking. "I don't understand what this has to do with me," I repeated.

Tricia looked only the slightest bit crestfallen as she gave a crisp nod and settled back into her chair. "All right. Let me lay it out for you like this. We're casting seven strangers to live in a house together. Each housemate has some degree of psychic ability, plus a unique personality trait that overwhelms the others. For example, one participant has anger management issues. We've cast him as Wrath. Another participant is a hoarder and doesn't like to clean up after herself. We've cast her in the role of Sloth. Envy is portrayed by a jealous young woman for whom the world is a profoundly unfair place. The other parts are still up for negotiation." She tilted her head to the side. "Including yours."

"Mine?" I leaned forward into the question, hand pressed to my chest. "You want me to live in a house with six strangers with personality defects while you film the whole thing?"

Tricia pointed a finger in my direction. "That's exactly what we want to do, yes."

"And which sin did you want me to play?"

Again, that movie-star smile. "Isn't it obvious? Pride."

It took me a minute to digest what she was saying, and I was probably staring at her like an idiot with my mouth falling open as I mulled this over. When my brain finally caught up to the conversation, I barked out a single laugh. "Is this some kind of joke?"

"I assure you, it's not. Now, our show differs from our Japanese inspiration in another important way. We are adding a competition aspect. We'll be sending you off in small groups to complete various challenges around town. Helping the elderly with household chores and errands, for example. This is all to engage the audience. And each week, the audience will vote on their favorite house members. At the end of the season, the audience favorite, determined by votes, will receive something special in return."

I leaned away from her, fidgeting in my seat. "Something special?"

Tricia cocked her head to the side, her eyes narrowing as the smile slipped from her lips. "Sid, what's the one thing you want more than anything else in the world?"

I answered without thinking. "I want my girlfriend Shayda back," I said.

"That's very noble," Tricia said. "And we can make that happen." Before I could ask how, Tricia reached across the table, pressing her palm against the white linen cloth. "You're the person for this part, Sid. I want the real deal. I want honest-to-God psychics, real witches, genuine summoners, the whole shebang. So we will reward you well. The winner will be granted their deepest true desire. There are some caveats, of course, which will be stipulated in your contract. But I assure you, this is all on the up-and-up. So what do you say, Sid? How'd you like to be famous?"

I stared at her, wondering where to start. She said she'd done her research, yet she didn't realize what little appeal celebrity held for me. Famous? I didn't want to be famous. I wanted my girlfriend back. And regardless of her promises, I couldn't see how a TV show could help me realize that goal.

"It looks like this meeting was a big waste of both our time," I said with a tight smile. "You don't want me for your show. I promise. And more importantly, I don't want to be on your show. I'm sure you'll find someone else to fill the role. This is Southern California, after all. Everyone here is a star in the making."

The woman opposite me sighed, blowing out her cheeks, her mouth twitching to one side. "I can see I chose the wrong tack. But think about it, Sid. This is a really great opportunity." When I didn't say anything, Tricia retrieved a business card from her purse and slid it across the table. "Don't answer now. Take a few days to think it over. When you decide, call me."

"I've already decided," I said, taking the card and slipping it away anyway. "I'm not interested."

But Tricia acted like she hadn't heard. "I'll pay for dinner on my way out. Please stay and enjoy the meal on the network. It's the least I could do for your time."

I was going to tell her how much I hated the phrase "It's the least I could do," because it made the person saying it sound lazy and ungracious. Why would anyone admit to doing the *least* they could do? But before I could say anything, Tricia was already on the other side of the dining room, and then she was gone.

three

. . .

The next day was Tuesday, which meant I had to go to work even though I'd worked all weekend and just wanted to sit in my near-empty apartment and sulk. When I arrived at the police station, Angela Richards, the city's head of HR, was sitting in the lobby. She was jittery, fidgeting with her hair and clothes, her leg bouncing up and down as she chewed her lips. I recognized those tells: Angela was nervous, but that wasn't any surprise. Angela always looked nervous. For someone whose job was dealing with people, she was horrible at it. Not as bad as me, but you expect more from a human resources person. Anyway, when she saw me, she stood up clumsily, her hands shaking as she reached for the necklace she wore at her throat, wrapping it around her fingers. You didn't need to be a detective to know something was up.

"Good morning, Sid." She donned a tight smile that didn't quite reach her eyes. "Have a good weekend?"

I frowned. "I worked all weekend. Angela, you know

I don't like small talk. What are you doing here? I have a meeting with Detective Hidalgo in 15 minutes."

Angela bobbed her head up and down, but it wasn't exactly a nod. It was more of a tick. "Yes, right. Well, that's what I wanted to talk to you about, Sid. Can we go someplace a bit more private?"

It wasn't really a question. She grabbed me by the elbow and led me down the hallway toward an empty office she was squatting in. I gently pried myself out of her grasp; I didn't really like touching other people if I didn't have to. Part of that is my anxiety and awkwardness, but it's also because sometimes when I touch people, I see things I don't want to see. Luckily, when Angela touched me, nothing happened.

When we were safely ensconced in her makeshift office, Angela closed the door and bid me sit at the desk. Stacked on top in three piles was paperwork I immediately recognized.

I looked up as my shoulders slouched. "Are you firing me?"

Angela offered me that same tight smile, but her eyes were cloudy. "Sid, I hope you know how much we appreciate you around here. I know it was hard getting the respect you deserve at first. We're a little behind the times when it comes to using psychics in our investigations, but the people who matter? They all recognize your genius. But the mayor's up for reelection soon, and he's made it clear he's not comfortable with the scrutiny the department's been getting because we consult with you. And, besides that, there've also been budget cuts." She said this last part as if it was supposed to soften the blow, but when you've just been fired, there's really no softening that. It all sucks.

"So you see, this is out of our hands. If we could keep you on, we would. But right now…" She let her voice trail off as she dropped her gaze and shrugged. "I'm really sorry, Sid. But we have to let you go."

Officially, I'd been working for the San Diego Police Department as a contractor. I was not a full-time employee, and so, in theory, all of this was unnecessary. They could've handled the termination of my contract with a simple phone call. Doing it this way was supposed to be an olive branch. I understood that. But I didn't like it. I would have preferred a phone call and saved the trip down here.

But this wasn't Angela's fault. She was just doing her job. So I shook myself off, cleared my throat, and nodded. "Yeah, I get it. I understand. I knew this gig wouldn't last forever, so it's okay, Angela. Really." It really wasn't, but sometimes even I had to say things I didn't mean. "So, do you need me to sign something, or…?"

Angela pushed the piles of paper toward me. "Well, these are for you. This one just says we're terminating the contract. You can look it over at your leisure. This one talks about how you're going to receive the remainder of your money. And this over here is just recommendation letters from the department. You know, in case you decide you want to take your services elsewhere. We're happy to recommend you to others."

"But you don't want to use me anymore yourself."

I shouldn't have said that, and I regretted it the

moment the words were out of my mouth. Angela turned an unsightly shade of pink as she tilted her head to the side, dropping her chin in her hand. "I hate this for you, Sid. I know how hard it is for you to get work. And you're really good at your job. I mean, just astoundingly good from what I hear. You realize this isn't personal, right?"

Of course I knew it wasn't personal. It was entirely professional, and that made it worse. Look, I could understand not wanting to be my friend. I knew I made people uncomfortable. But Angela was right about one thing—I was really good at my job. So I would rather hear that the department was getting rid of me because I creeped people out than because my work was deemed unnecessary or unsavory.

"I solved the Maryann Holder case," I said, almost to myself. "I was the one that found the ghost in the parking garage. I was the one that asked the ghost what it saw. You know how unusual it is to have a ghost as the only eyewitness? No one else in the department could've gotten that information. It was me."

Angela was nodding and swiping at her nose. I couldn't tell if she was about to cry—her tells weren't the same as Shayda's. Still, she was making me anxious.

"And the Marco Gilmore murder? I found the key evidence in that case, too. Doesn't the mayor care about that? Or *all* the other crimes this department solved because of my abilities?"

Angela looked up at me, her eyes melty and downward tilting. "What do you want me to say? This wasn't my decision. Nobody really wants you out of here, but—"

I held up a hand. "Number one, that's not true. Plenty of people really want me out of here. But number two, I get what you're saying. I don't mean to make this difficult for you. I should go."

I gathered up the papers without looking at them and rose to my feet. I was already halfway to the door when I stopped and turned around. "It was nice working with you, Angela. Maybe we'll keep in touch?"

I don't know why I made it a question. I wasn't even sure I wanted her to keep in touch. What did I think might happen? We'd meet for coffee on Wednesday afternoons? Go out for drinks on Saturday nights? I couldn't see any of that happening. But that was the sort of thing people said when they separated from a job, right? That whole keep in touch thing?

I felt stupid as soon as I said it. So instead of waiting for a response, I shouldered my way out the door.

———

When I got home, I saw that Shayda had been back. More of her things were gone, including much of the furniture. I wasn't sure how she managed to move so much furniture in the short amount of time I was gone, but then I didn't think about it too hard, either.

She left a note on the refrigerator. All it said was, "Pay the rent."

That's when the reality of everything happening really hit home.

Shayda was an obstetrics nurse practitioner, and she made good money. That was how we afforded this apartment in San Diego. I never could've lived here on my own. Hell, even between the two of us, making ends meet was rough. But when you have a good attitude and a partner who loves and supports you, you can do almost anything.

(I don't know why I just said that. I must've read that on a greeting card. Or maybe I heard Dr. Xena say it. That cockamamie nonsense wouldn't have naturally come from my brain.)

But anyway, I had neither a good attitude nor a partner who loved and supported me. I was a loner who had just been dumped and fired, so that meant I could do pretty much nothing.

Especially pay the rent on an apartment in San Diego.

(Those thoughts were my own. That's precisely the kind of depressing thing my brain would come up with.)

I plucked the note from the refrigerator and stared at it, my mind running through the possibilities. I could call the landlord and explain my situation, but I wasn't sure that would do any good. After all, if I were the landlord, I would shrug off that sob story and start my search for a brand-new wealthy tenant.

Plus, admitting my dire straits was something I could never, ever do.

Realizing that was a dead end, I considered other options. I could get a quick temp job, though I wasn't sure what I was qualified to temp at that would pay anything close to supporting a lovely apartment a few miles from the beach. I could sell plasma, but again, while I might be able to scrape together enough money for a seafood dinner, rent was probably out of the question. I could ask Shayda for the money, but I would rather die than put myself in her debt.

That wasn't hyperbole, either. If I had a choice between begging my ex-girlfriend for money or lying in the middle of Pacific Coast Highway, I'd be face-down on the freeway before you could say "6-car pileup."

I'm not suicidal. But I do have my limits.

I thought about calling my therapist. In times like these, getting advice from a professional might not be the worst idea in the world. But just as I didn't want to ask for help from Shayda, I also didn't want to ask Dr. Xena for help. I realized that was stupid. Asking an ex-girlfriend for help is one thing; asking your therapist for help is another. Dr. Xena got paid to help me with difficult situations.

Or at least, she did.

Dr. Xena was part of my health insurance. Health insurance I got through Shayda. And now that I didn't have Shayda, I probably wouldn't have insurance much longer, either.

It's a hell of a thing to realize in one afternoon that everything you used to take for granted was gone.

I crumbled up the Post-it note and threw it in the trash. I couldn't pay the rent. That was a no-go, so it didn't make sense to waste time thinking about it anymore. I was out of options. I wouldn't ask Shayda for help. I couldn't go to Dr. Xena. The city had let me down.

And then, just as I was about to make my way down to the local bar to drown my worries in a gin and tonic, I thought of Tricia Woodward and her pretty linen dress and her sensible shoes and her mysterious smile.

No way, I thought, shaking my head even at the idea. *I'm not calling the network. Absolutely not. No, no, no—*

"Hey."

The voice startled me. I looked up to find a girl standing just a few feet away from me, arms akimbo, her dimpled face smiling out from underneath a mass of thick, chocolate-brown hair. She ambled toward me and climbed up on the couch, curling up in the corner, hugging her knees to her chest. "Whatcha doin'?"

I smiled at her, oddly comforted that she'd chosen now to appear. It was a ghost girl—but not just any ghost girl. She was the very first ghost I'd ever seen, and now I'd been seeing her my whole life. When she first appeared, we were roughly the same age. Over time, I'd grown up.

She never did.

The first time I saw her, she'd appeared in my front yard while I was spying on the neighbors with a pair of orange plastic binoculars I'd gotten for Christmas. She was wearing a pink t-shirt and khaki shorts, the same outfit she'd wear for the rest of our lives together. Anyway, that first day, she surprised me by approaching from behind, tugging on the hem of my t-shirt. When I spun around, she cocked her head to the side and asked innocently, "Whatcha doin'?"

I stammered, lowering the binoculars to my side. "Nothing. Just playing," I said.

The girl pointed to my binoculars. "Can I try?"

I wasn't sure I should insinuate anyone else in my illicit activities. Still, even as a child, I was lonely, and the idea of sharing my covert operation was appealing. Besides, the neighbors weren't naked or anything. They were just sitting around watching television. So I shrugged in agreement. She held out her hand, but when I dropped the binoculars into her open palm, they clattered to the ground.

"Hey!" I shrieked. "You gotta be careful with those! If they break, I probably won't get another pair."

I bent over to retrieve the toy, and when I stood up, the girl was gone.

I leaned back into the sofa, digging my knuckles into my eye sockets. "Now isn't a good time," I said. "What do you want?"

The ghost sucked her teeth. "You just seem sad is all. I thought maybe I could make you feel better. Did you know you can hear a blue whale's heartbeat from miles away?"

I sighed. The ghost loved to tell me random facts, especially about wildlife. She'd been doing it for as long as I'd known her. "I didn't know that."

"It's true. And did you know that crocodiles are over 200 million years old?"

"I don't think that's true," I said. "No creature can live for 200 million years."

The ghost rolled her eyes. "I mean, crocodiles have been on *Earth* for that long."

I shrugged. "That's not what you said."

"You knew what I meant. And did you know mantis

shrimps have sixteen cones in their eyes, while humans only have three? They can see colors we can't even imagine."

"That one I did know," I said. "You've told me before."

The ghost pretended not to hear. "I learned all that in school."

I shook my head. "You haven't been to school in a really long time. Why do you keep hanging around here, anyway? Nobody else seems to want anything to do with me." I realized as I said the words that I sounded pathetic, which I hated, so I changed tacks. "Don't you have other people you can haunt?"

That made her laugh. "I'm not haunting you, silly. I just want to know what you're doing. I thought maybe we could play a game."

I let out a long sigh. "We've tried to play lots of games, but you can't touch things. You can't handle a video game controller, you can't move pieces around a board…Hell, you can't even skip rope. We've tried all these things, remember? I don't even understand how you're sitting on the couch right now. How come you don't just fall right through?"

She wound a stray lock of dark hair around her finger. "Yeah, I don't know. You're right about the games. But maybe we could play something like a guessing game? There's no pieces to touch in that. I could think of a number, and you could try to guess it."

I squinted at her. "A guessing game? I have a similar idea. Why don't you tell me your name?"

Now, the ghost looked sullen. "I thought we weren't

gonna do this anymore," she said. "I've told you a million times. I can only tell you my name if you tell me yours."

It was true. She had told me this particular rule of hers at least a million times. Well, probably not a million, because that's a really large number, but a lot of times, anyway. What I didn't understand was:

1. Why she was so adamant about this rule, and
2. Why she thought I hadn't already told her my name. Because I had, at least a million times. Or maybe not exactly a million. But you know what I'm saying.

"My name is Sidney Sheridan," I said for the million-and-first time. "I don't have a middle name. What else do you want to know?"

The ghost sighed and dropped her face low, pressing her cheek against her knees. "That's not your real name, though. And if you won't tell me your real name, why should I tell you mine?"

I threw up my hands. "Fine. Don't tell me your name. But, honestly, I'm not in the mood for this today. You know what rent is?"

The girl shook her head. "Sounds like some kind of boring grown-up stuff."

"Yeah, you got that right," I chuckled. "Boring grown-up stuff. Well, right now, I have to worry about my rent. And a lot of other really boring grown-up stuff."

The ghost was peering at me quizzically. "Like what?"

I sucked in a breath. "Like whether I'm going to sell my soul to the devil."

"That sounds scary," she said, making bug eyes at me.

I thought of Tricia Woodward's offer and the idea of living on camera with six strangers, each with psychic abilities and an array of personality flaws and shook my head in real horror. "Ghostie, you don't even know the half of it."

Then I picked up my phone.

four

. . .

Two weeks later, I was standing outside an ostentatious ocean-side home with my suitcase in hand. I felt like a schmuck. Not only was I carrying a mostly empty bag, pretending like I was moving into this house for the first time, but I was really about to do this. I was really about to walk into this house filled with cameras and start a "new life" with a bunch of psychologically questionable strangers. Thinking about it this way almost sent me into a panic attack, so I closed my eyes and counted backward from 10 while I thought about comforting things. The way Shayda smelled after she'd been painting. The taste of champagne. The way reading my favorite book made me feel. Pretty soon, I was feeling better, but I still didn't want to go inside. Even so, it was too late for second thoughts. Not only had I already signed a contract, but I had no other place to live, no money, no job, and no other options.

Sucking in a deep breath, I strode toward the door,

threw my shoulders back, and pressed the buzzer. A moment later, a female voice answered. "Hello?"

I forced a fake friendliness into my voice. "I'm the new housemate. I'm moving in today."

I heard giggling on the other end, and then the door buzzed open.

With my weighted suitcase in hand, I entered my new home. I'd been here before to drop off my belongings, but I hadn't actually seen the place since it had been furnished.

It was sleek, minimal, and modern. Everything was white: the walls, the tile floors, the ceiling. Enormous windows overlooked the Pacific Ocean, and tall, potted plants luxuriated in the sunlight. Tasteful paintings decorated the walls, and throw rugs made the place feel inviting instead of sterile.

It was almost welcoming until I noticed the cameramen.

I wasn't supposed to look at them, of course. The whole point of the show was to appear as natural as possible. Still, each time I caught a glimpse of the lenses or the blinking "Recording" lights from the corner of an eye, I felt a chill run down my spine.

What had I gotten myself into?

As I was taking all of this in, a pair of women appeared.

They were smiling like schoolgirls. One of them reached her hand out to me, and I accepted as I set my suitcase on the floor. "So you're the new housemate," she said, a crooked smile curling over her lips. "You're the last one to arrive!"

My eyebrows shot up. "Oh, really?" I glanced around. "Where's everyone else?"

"Down at the beach, probably," one of them said with a slight frown. "I wish I had that level of carefree, wild abandon! Must be so nice to have a body you can just flaunt in front of God and country without even giving it a second thought!"

Without meaning to, I let my eyes travel the length of the woman's body. I didn't see anything wrong with it.

"You must be Pride," she said. "I'm Envy. It's nice to meet you."

The other woman waved without offering her hand. "I'm Sloth."

Although we'd all been prepped on how to address each other, hearing these women address themselves by presumably their biggest flaw was *weird*. Can you imagine some very normal-looking person walking up to you, extending their hand, and saying, "Hi, I'm Pathological Liar!" How would you respond to that? It was jarring, is what I'm saying.

But then I remembered the cameras, so I pushed the thought away and grinned. "Nice to meet you, too." I gestured toward my fake luggage. "So, where should I put this?"

"Your room's upstairs," Envy said, nodding toward the staircase. "You want me to show you around? We all have our own rooms. This place is *huge*. My room is okay, but it doesn't overlook the water like *yours* does. God, I *wish* I had your room. Let me know if you want to trade."

Sloth came forward then, holding out a hand. "Here, why don't you give me your stuff? I'll put it in your room while Envy gives you a tour."

I looked down to see Sloth's hand covered in something red and sticky. She must've caught me looking because she giggled and rushed to explain. "It's just melted popsicle," she said. "Just sugar. It'll wash right off. I promise not to get any on your stuff."

I wasn't so sure she could keep that promise, but I also knew this was part of the routine. The cameras were going to follow me and Envy around the house while Sloth took my fake suitcase to my already-prepared room. So I handed the other woman my luggage. She gave me a military salute as Envy grabbed me by the elbow.

At her touch, images flashed before my eyes. A fiery lizard, a nondescript humanoid composed of water, a short humanoid that could only be described as a gnome, and a wispy humanoid that looked to be cast in smoke. Abruptly, I yanked my arm free of Envy's grasp. The woman looked at me, her eyes betraying the slightest smile as she glanced almost imperceptibly in the camera's direction. "Is something wrong?" she asked.

"Not wrong," I drawled, rubbing the spot on my arm where she'd touched me. "But sometimes when people touch me, I see things."

Envy cocked an eyebrow. "Did you see something just now?"

I swallowed. "Yes. I saw…Well, I don't really know how to describe it. I saw four creatures surrounding you.

Creatures made of air and water. A little guy, like a gnome. And a lizard made of fire."

A slow smile spread over Envy's mouth, and she popped a hand on her hip, her head listing to one side. "Interesting! I'm gonna have to keep my eye on you. Well, you'll get to know those guys soon enough, I guess. They sort of follow me around. Are you familiar with the four cardinal elements? Earth, air, water, fire?"

My eyes narrowed. "Sure, I guess." I wasn't, though. Not really. But neither she nor all of America needed to know the depths of my ignorance.

"Well, each cardinal element is represented by a different being. Elementals, some people call them. I guess you could say I have an affinity for them. They come and go as they please, of course, but sometimes, I can convince them to do some simple tasks. If they feel like it."

I wanted to ask more questions, but I saw that Envy was deliberately ending this conversation. She was trying to follow Tricia's directives. We weren't supposed to talk about our abilities. We were only supposed to *show* the audience what we could do—but only in a natural, everyday kind of way, whatever that meant.

"Okay, so this is obviously the kitchen. Get a load of these appliances. I mean, top of the line. I hope some-body here turns out to be a great cook. I can't cook at all, but I love to eat. I have to keep an eye on that, though. You know what I'm saying? It's so unfair how some people can eat anything they want, and the rest of us have to watch every single calorie, or else we'll blow up like a giant Pillsbury Doughboy. So where are you from?"

The subject change threw me for a loop, and I blinked back my surprise. "Here," I said. "Well, San Diego. You?"

"Pittsburgh. There's one other person here from California, but I can't remember who. Maybe you two know each other."

I couldn't tell if that was supposed to be a joke or not. California is one of the biggest states in the country, with a population of almost 40 million. So the odds of knowing another random Californian were slim. Only an idiot wouldn't realize that, and I wasn't sure whether Envy was an idiot, so I decided to give her the benefit of the doubt and treated her statement as a joke. I chuckled. I must have guessed right because she grinned and motioned with her head for me to follow her.

We exited the kitchen and walked through the main living room to a second open area with the dartboard, a pool table, beanbag chairs, the whole nine yards. It looked like a scene from a frat house movie. "Okay, and this is the recreation room. Haven't spent any time in here yet. But I mean, we all just got here, so. Do you play darts?"

I shook my head. "No. Do you?"

She wrinkled her nose. "No. Who the heck plays darts? I heard we might get a foosball table, but I'm not super interested in that, either."

We left the room, and Envy continued the tour. In addition to the recreation room, the house also featured a theater room, a unisex bath and sauna, beach access, a pool, and half a dozen bathrooms. "Apparently, this place used to be a beach condo," Envy explained. "But I guess it's been recently renovated to be a private house. Can you believe we really get to live here?"

Under different circumstances, I'm sure I would have been just as enthralled with the space as she was. But all I could think about was how Shayda would have hung her paintings in the kitchen, replacing the generic "Taco Tuesday" sign hanging in there now. I thought about how the house would smell faintly of floral perfume, especially after Shayda came out of the shower. But I pulled the best smile I could out of my hat and nodded. "It's amazing," I agreed.

"Well, I probably ought to let you get upstairs and get settled in," Envy said. "God only knows what Sloth is doing with your things. You better go up there and kick her out before she gets popsicle juice all over your walls or something."

I fake laughed as my stomach flipped over. Just thinking about that woman rifling through my things was enough to give me hives. "Ok, cool. Hey, thanks for the tour."

"No problem. When you get bored, come find me. Maybe we can go find a café and get a bite to eat or something? The fridge is still empty. Some of the others wanted to get the shopping out of the way earlier, but Wrath and I voted to wait until you got here."

I squinted. "Two out of six people won the vote?"

Envy chuckled. "Oh, right. You haven't met Wrath yet."

I watched in silence as Envy disappeared around a

corner. I glanced surreptitiously at the cameraman, who was swallowing down a chuckle.

Heat rose in my cheeks. *What the hell have I gotten myself into?*

five

· · ·

"**G**ood morning, everyone! And welcome to your first official day at *Sinful House!*"

Tricia Woodward was dressed in a simple gray cotton shift, her hair pulled into a neat ponytail. She was too chipper for 8 o'clock in the morning. We were sitting in a semicircle around her in the main living room. Some of us were drinking coffee; others were rubbing the sleep from our eyes as we tried to hide our yawns. I was in the second group. It seemed that none of us were morning people, and for some reason, that made me feel better.

"As you all know, I'm here to give you your assignments this morning. You will be working in teams to help out various members of the local community. The teams were assigned beforehand, but each team will randomly select an assignment from the pot. You have two weeks to complete your task. After that, we'll assign new teams and challenges. There's no penalty for failing a task. But each completed challenge grants 'Good

Samaritan' points. You get more points the earlier you complete your challenge. Your Good Samaritan points will be added to your Audience Favorite votes at the end of the season. We encourage every team to try their best." She flashed us a bright smile. "Any questions so far?"

No one said anything. We all knew the drill.

Tricia clapped her hands together. "Great! Then let's go ahead and get started." She retrieved a piece of paper sitting in front of her on the coffee table. "The teams are as follows: Team one is Pride and Lust. Team two is Greed and Wrath. And team three is Envy, Gluttony, and Sloth."

One of the men in the semicircle rose to his feet, hands balled into fists at his side. "What the hell? Right off the bat, the teams are unfair? Why does team three have three people and the rest of us only have two?"

Tricia's head listed to one side. "That's a great question, Wrath. But as I'm sure you can tell, seven doesn't divide neatly. Every week, one team will have three people. But don't worry. Having that extra person might not be as much of a boon as you expect. Sometimes, the more people we have to work with, the harder it can be to reach consensus and make decisions."

This didn't assuage Wrath, whose face darkened as he approached the producer. "This is rigged," he said, pointing a finger in her face. "You need to fix this, or I'll call my agent. Get an additional housemate if you have to."

"Are you stupid or something?" This comment came from another man in the group. He was tall and lean, with dark hair that brushed against his shoulders. His features were sharp, his eyes bright. "There are *seven* deadly sins, you dolt. Not eight."

"Greed's right," Envy said. "There's seven of us, and that's how it has to be. You'll just have to accept that."

Greed and Wrath shot daggers at each other before Wrath sucked in a breath and returned to his seat, face red, nostrils still flared. "I still say this is rigged," he muttered.

Now, Tricia looked to me, her hands folded in her lap as she leaned forward. "Pride, as the last person to arrive, you get to choose the first mission." She pointed to a wicker basket sitting on the table between us. "Go ahead and make your selection. But do me a favor and don't look until everyone has chosen their assignment."

I did as I was told, retrieving a paper from the basket. My skin prickled over at the feeling of everyone's eyes on me. I didn't like being the center of attention, which was pretty stupid considering I was now on a reality TV show where my every move would be broadcast to homes all across America. I ignored the cameras with the "Recording" lights that blinked in the background and sat back down.

The other teams chose their assignments, and when the basket was empty, Tricia leaned back and crossed her legs. "All right! Everyone, please find your teammate and see what you got. You're free to begin your task immediately. If you get stuck, you can ask other teams for help. But of course, no one is obligated to help you. I wish you all the best of luck, and may the best Sins win!"

Everyone got to their feet. I glanced around the room, unsure which of the remaining people I didn't know was Lust. I'd already met the short, round-cheeked girl with hay-colored pigtails and peaches and cream skin: that was Sloth. I also ruled out the pasty, wiry dude with sharp eyes: that was Greed. Wrath was the handsome but volatile Asian fellow with bleached blond hair, and Envy was the girl-next-door woman who'd given me a tour of the house.

So that left two people I hadn't met: Lust and Gluttony.

It didn't take long to figure out who was who. A tall woman approached me, raven hair undone and tumbling in loose curls. She wore an off-the-shoulder t-shirt that revealed smooth, cinnamon-brown skin and cut-offs so short they left nothing to the imagination. Even at this hour, her face was painted to perfection, and she sauntered over to me with the grace of a cat on the prowl. She placed a hand on my forearm. Strangely, I didn't want to pull away. "We didn't get a chance to meet yesterday," she said. Her voice was both husky and melodious. "I'm Lust."

I cleared my throat. "Pride," I said, extending a hand. "Nice to meet you."

"Likewise. So." She glanced at the paper in my hand. "Should we go ahead and see what the network has in store for us?"

Obediently, I unfolded the paper. Lust peered over my shoulder, and I read the contents aloud for the cameras. "Help Linda and Eric Wong discover who's been tampering with their fortune cookies."

I looked up, my brow creased in confusion. "That's it? There's no address or phone number or anything."

Lust took the paper from my fingers, flipped it over to confirm, then folded it and slipped it in my pocket. "Well, my guess is they own a Chinese restaurant, so maybe we start there."

Lust whipped a phone from a pocket. She tapped in a Google search and, after a quick browse, snapped her fingers in victory. "Aha. Here we go. There's a story from the Odyssey News website about a Chinese restaurant having trouble with pranksters altering the fortune cookies. Apparently, the locals are pretty mad about it."

"Okay. What's the name of the restaurant?"

Lust shoved the phone in my face before announcing aloud, "Wights and Wongs." She chuckled, a throaty sound that made my spine tingle. "Oh man, that's good. That's *funny.*"

"Why's it funny?"

Lust peered at me a moment before answering. "Well, it's a pun, sweetie. Like Rights and Wrongs, but Wights and Wongs? Get it?"

I didn't get it, but I wasn't going to admit that. So instead, I said, "I wonder why they named it that."

Lust looked back down at her phone before answering. "Probably because it's owned by the Wong family and—get this—they don't have human servers. All their food is served by ghosts—wights, to be exact."

"Oh." That was a twist I hadn't expected. "Technically, wights aren't ghosts," I mused aloud. "Ghosts are spirits of dead people. Wights are cursed, immortal spirits forced to wander the Earth in never-ending servitude."

"*Okay*, Professor Freak Show! Hey, don't me wrong, knowledge is sexy. Keep those random factoids coming. Just not right now, though," she said, interrupting the speech I was about to give about various kinds of earth-bound spirits. "We should get going. I don't know about you, but I'm not about to lose to any of these other clowns. What do you say? Are you in the mood for some moo goo gai pan?"

I gestured over my shoulder with my thumb. "I thought we were going to help the Wongs figure out—"

Lust barked a laugh, her eyes wide. "Wow, you're super literal, aren't you? Come on, Freak Show. Let's go solve the fortune cookie caper."

six

. . .

Wights and Wongs was on the other side of town but still only a ten-minute drive from the house. Unlike other Chinese restaurants tucked away in strip malls, Wights and Wongs was an ornate standalone building designed to look like a Chinese palace. The exterior was red and black, with an ornate tiled roof adorned with stone dragon guardians. A lighted path led up to double front doors that swung open easily despite their size.

Stepping through the doorway was like entering another world. The eerie sounds of wind whistling through trees and somber organ music drifted from unseen speakers. The inside was dark, lit by strategically placed red candles. The walls were adorned with paintings featuring dark, moody scenes from a forest where specters peeked out from behind gnarled trees. The combined effect of lighting, art, and music was fantastic and unlike anything I expected. Whoever designed this place was a genius. A bit twisted, maybe, but a genius.

Standing behind a podium, a bored hostess, no older than eighteen, hardly looked up from her seating chart. She wore a vintage graphic t-shirt with the words "Save the whales!" splashed across the front. "Welcome to Wights and Wongs. How many?"

I cleared my throat. "Actually, we're looking for Linda or Eric Wong? Are they here by any chance?"

The girl looked up, and when she saw the cameramen behind us, her eyes went wide, and her hands flew to her mouth. "Oh my gosh! You must be those people from that show! I heard you were coming today, but I totally forgot! Oh my gosh, am I going to be on television?" Her cheeks turned an alarming shade of red as she tittered, shifting her weight from foot to foot and combing her fingers through her long, dark hair. "No, don't tell me. I know I'm doing this all wrong. I'm supposed to pretend like the cameras aren't here and stuff, right? Well, I guess they can edit this part out. I'm such a moron! Okay. Let me start over."

The girl shook herself, arranged her hair around her shoulders without obscuring the lettering on her shirt. Then she looked up, a bright smile on her face. "Hi! Welcome to Wights and Wongs! How many will be dining with us today?"

I choked down a chuckle at her acting job. She certainly had a future in the spotlight if she wanted it. "We're here to see Linda or Eric Wong. Are they available?"

The girl brought an index finger to her chin, tapping lightly as she pretended to think. "Yes, I think they're both in the back. Would you like to be seated, and I can have them join you when they're ready?"

Lust nodded. "Sure. Sounds great."

The girl stepped out from behind the podium with menus in hand and motioned for us to follow her. "Excellent. Right this way."

As we wended our way through the restaurant, I noticed how empty the place was. It was lunchtime, and I expected the place to be bustling. But as we walked through the main dining hall, I noticed at least 80 percent of the tables were vacant. I elbowed Lust in the side. "Place is pretty empty. No way they can cover their overhead with a crowd like this. You think they do most of their business at dinner?"

Lust leaned in to answer. "Could be. But I have a feeling the lack of customers has something to do with the fortune cookie shenanigans."

Upon hearing the words 'fortune cookie,' the hostess turned around. "It's really awful what's been happening here," she said. "Mom and Dad are really torn up about it. I hope you guys can get to the bottom of it. Okay, here we go." She'd led us to a private room large enough to seat eight people. The cameramen ensconced themselves in the corners where they could shoot the whole room from different angles. I chose a seat facing the door, and to my surprise, Lust chose to sit beside me rather than across. She was so close, I felt her thigh pressing against mine.

The hostess handed us our menus and said, "A wight will be with you shortly." Then she excused herself and disappeared down the dim corridor.

Lust whistled as she looked around the room. "This place is wild," she said. "Have you ever seen anything like this? I feel like I'm at some haunted amusement park ride."

She was right. Our private room boasted a chandelier that was professionally designed to look like it hadn't been dusted in about 20 years. Artificial cobwebs glittered on the ceiling. The art on the walls featured graveyards with shrines in the background. But the chairs were comfortable, the table didn't wobble when you leaned on it, and there were real linen napkins for place settings.

I barely had a chance to peruse the menu—which was extensive—before two people entered our room.

They were both Asian. The woman was tall and severe, with thin lips and long, dark hair. The man with her was shorter and more relaxed, with wire-rimmed glasses and hair styled away from a broad, handsome face. They were both dressed simply in slacks and button-down shirts.

"Hello," the woman said, tucking a stray lock of hair behind her ear. "Thank you for coming. I'm Linda Wong." The woman shook hands with Lust first, then me. "It's nice to meet you."

"I'm Lust," my companion said, one hand placed on her chest. "And this is my friend, Pride."

Linda gestured toward the man with her. "This is my husband, Eric. You already met our daughter, Ruby." The Wongs slid into their seats beside us, their hands folded on the table. "How would you like to begin?" Linda asked.

I shrugged. "We don't know anything about what's been going on here. So how about starting from the beginning?"

Eric nodded, clearing his throat as he adjusted in his seat. "It all began a few weeks ago. I'd gotten a new shipment of fortune cookies. We get them from a company up in San Francisco. We've been ordering from the same place for years. Never had a problem. Anyway, our sous chef, Ping Lau, sent the fortune cookies to Table 31 just as she normally would. Later that night, our daughter, Ruby, who was hosting, received a complaint from one of our guests. The guest's name was Charmaine Young. She said her fortune was inappropriate."

My brow wrinkled. "Inappropriate how?"

"Well, you know how fortune cookies are. They usually say dumb, innocuous things like, *'You are the life of the party.'* Or sometimes they give actual fortunes like, *'Expect a windfall of money coming your way soon.'* But Charmaine claimed her fortune said, *'A dark horse rides at midnight, bringing an untimely death to the family.'*"

Lust and I exchanged looks. "That is grim," Lust said, propping her cheek against a fist. "Then what happened?"

"Well, she showed the fortune to Ruby, but when Ruby looked at it, the fortune read, *'The best gift you can give is your smile.'* Charmaine was furious, claiming Ruby was lying, and she demanded to speak to us." Eric gestured between himself and his wife. "When we read the fortune, we saw what Ruby saw."

"I assumed she was nuts or just trying to get a

comped meal," Linda admitted. "The fortune obviously didn't say what that woman claimed it said. But then…"

The Wongs glanced at each other before looking down at the table, their cheeks coloring red. "Less than a week later, that woman's uncle passed away. He was the mayor of the next town over."

A chill ran down my spine. "So the fortune came true," I said. "Probably just a fluke, though, right?"

Linda sucked in a breath. "Well, that's what we thought, too. But unfortunately, the awful fortunes continued. One woman got a fortune predicting layoffs at her company, and days later, she was let go. Another patron was told to expect heartbreak. His wife filed for divorce. So as you can see, it's not just that the fortunes are dark and only appear to the person they're destined for. It's that they're also accurate."

Lust murmured a thinking sound as she absently stroked a lock of hair. "Very strange, indeed."

"After that, we checked the cookie shipment," Eric said. "Ruby and I opened about thirty fortune cookies, and none of them said anything bad. Just the same old stuff. Still, we threw the rest of the batch away, and my wife called our vendor to complain. They sent us a replacement batch for free. When they arrived, we went through those the same way, opening a couple dozen at random, and they seemed untainted. But…" Eric sighed, shaking his head miserably. "That night, one of Ruby's friends, Lee Jordan, got a fortune that said, 'Troublesome times await you. Expect family to be detained against their will.' And sure enough—"

"Lee's dad was arrested for money laundering and

other fraud," Linda finished. "After that, journalists got a hold of the story. Charmaine Young was on every news station crying about how we cursed her uncle. She was in the papers. And she grew a following, too. Thanks to her, people stayed away."

I folded my arms over my chest. "I guess I can see how this might be a problem."

"This is our family business," Eric said, his voice strained. "It's our income. Our livelihood. Ruby is about to graduate high school. Soon, we'll have to pay for college. But people don't want to eat here anymore. The idea of inviting a curse freaks them out. And I can't say I blame them."

I was opening my mouth to suggest that diners who didn't want to know their future shouldn't eat fortune cookies when the air in the room suddenly chilled. I looked over to find that an apparition had materialized at the side of our table. At first glance, it looked like a pillar of swirling smoke. But soon, I realized the shifting image was that of a skeletal figure wrapped in a gauzy, hooded cloak, its eyes glowing with a green, lambent glow.

My breath caught. It was a wight. An actual, honest to God wight.

And it seemed to be waiting to take our orders.

"Combination lo mein for the table, please," Eric said to the wight. Then, reconsidering, he glanced around the table, eyebrows raised. "That's our house specialty, but if someone wants something else…"

Both Lust and I shook our heads. "Combination lo mein sounds great," I said.

"Egg rolls, too," Eric amended. He waved his hand, and the wight vanished.

"That's a hell of a trick," I said. "Never visited a haunted Chinese restaurant before. How did that happen, anyway?"

Linda sighed, running a hand through her hair. "It was my grandmother's fault," she said, a bit of ice in her voice. "When Eric and I first opened our restaurant, we didn't anticipate how expensive it would be to run. We were in danger of going under when I complained to my grandmother. She's a busybody, and in retrospect, I should've known better than to open my mouth. But I guess I'm glad I did. We certainly would have gone out of business if I hadn't."

At this, Eric's expression darkened. "Still, it was something we should've discussed together."

This was obviously an old argument, and Linda only rolled her eyes in response. "A few days later, my grandmother offered me a gift. She said it was a blessing she'd bought off a shaman recommended by one of her friends. She told me if I read the blessing in the middle of the restaurant, we'd receive an influx of money." Linda gave a dry, bitter chuckle. "That's how desperate I was, you see. I'm not superstitious. I don't really believe in those old Chinese blessings. Some people obviously have inexplicable abilities, but that's directed. Purposeful. I don't see how the universe just randomly bestows blessings on someone because they read words off a piece of paper."

"The universe is stranger than you imagine," Lust said.

"Hmm. Maybe." Linda frowned and smoothed her hair away from her face. "In any case, like an idiot, I read the blessing. Except it wasn't a blessing, and Grandmother didn't buy it from a shaman. It was a curse, which she bought from a disreputable curse vendor."

At my side, Lust chuckled. "Are there reputable curse vendors?"

Linda shrugged. "I don't know. Anyway, I was cursed from that moment to be haunted by twelve hungry wights. I don't know if you know this, but wights are bound spirits forced to spend eternity as servants." I did know that, but I let her keep talking. "They don't have free will, and they're immortal. So my grandmother cursed me with a lifetime of free labor, which was her way of solving our overhead problem. I'm still not sure how I feel about it," she admitted. "Anyway, when word got out that our food was served by ghosts, we became a curiosity. People came from all over to see our spirits. We had our fair share of people who tried to debunk us, of course. Some reporter from the next town even accused us of piping hallucinogens through the air vents to make people *think* they saw ghosts." Again, she rolled her eyes. "But over time, the *food* kept people coming back. Our sous chef, Ping, is a *miracle*. I don't think we could have done it without her. It wasn't long before we almost couldn't keep up with the demand. Our little restaurant was full to bursting every day."

"That's right," Eric said, nodding. "Within a year, we had enough money to upgrade. We left that little store in the strip mall, upgraded our appliances, and bought this place. Business has been booming ever since." His shoulders drooped, and he sighed, deflated. "Well, until recently."

An idea struck me, and I leaned forward onto my elbows. "I'm guessing some of the other local restaurants weren't too happy about your success," I said. "They might have reason to sabotage your business. Anybody in particular you think might be up to no good?"

Linda pursed her lips together, her eyes downcast. "Helen Park," she said. "She's been giving us trouble for years. She isn't even Chinese. She's Korean. She has a Chinese restaurant a couple of blocks away. Until recently, she hadn't been able to compete with us. But now, with everything going on here, she's doing better. Her business is picking up. I wouldn't be surprised if she had something to do with it."

Eric, however, didn't look convinced. "Helen Park has indeed been troublesome in the past, but I don't think she would do something like this. She has nothing against us personally. In fact, she's been teaching our daughter piano since she was a kindergartener. I can't imagine she would try to put us out of business, knowing the effect that would have on our daughter."

"And that right there is your problem," Linda said, turning to face her husband. "You always see the best in people. Just because Helen is nice to Ruby doesn't mean she wouldn't turn on her in a moment to save herself. I wouldn't put anything past that woman." Linda faced me, her eyes ablaze. "You should start there. She has to know something."

The room's temperature shifted again, and this time,

a half dozen wights appeared at the table with our order. Four of the wights carried platters of noodles while the other two had plates of egg rolls. They set our food before us and then drifted from the table, lingering shoulder to shoulder (if wights had shoulders) in a straight line. Eric offered the wights a tight flick of his fingers. "Thank you, that's all."

One by one, the wights silently disappeared.

Lust pressed her fingertips to her lips. "This really is spectacular," she breathed. "Even if people are getting fortune cookies they don't like, wouldn't they still want to come see this in person? I know I would."

Linda shrugged. "Newcomers and tourists, sure. But most of our business is the locals. They've seen this before. For them, the novelty wore off a while ago. They come for the food. Or did, anyway. So you see the problem."

"We'll look into Helen Park," I said, taking a tentative bite of steaming hot noodles. They were fantastic. I could see why this place had become locally famous. "Anyone else who might want to see you suffer?"

"There are plenty of people who would like to see this place disappear," Linda said with a frown. "The conservation groups have picketed here several times, claiming our property sits too close to the coastal lagoon, which is the habitat for the endangered…What is it? The freshwater gimlet?"

"Tidewater goby," her husband supplied.

"Right. Tidewater goby." She rolled her eyes, shaking her head. "And then there's the entire city council, which is full of racists. But if you ask me, the person doing this wants our *business*. There are other Chinese restaurants in town besides Helen's, but most of their business is delivery. Helen Park is the only person directly profiting from this fiasco."

Now, Lust leaned forward, drumming her nails on the table. "What about your grandmother?"

Linda's brow creased. "What about her?"

"Could she have anything to do with this? If she had access to a curse vendor to purchase a dozen eldritch servants, maybe she has the power to conjure up cursed fortune cookies, too."

"No." Linda folded her arms and shook her head. "Grandmother wouldn't do anything like that. Why would she? She spent a lot of money to help us become successful. Curses aren't cheap," she pointed out.

"Besides." Eric sighed heavily. "She's dead."

Just then, a wight appeared at our table bearing a tray of fortune cookies. It placed the tray in the center of the table and then vanished into thin air.

Discomfort washed over me as I stared at the tray. I looked up to meet Linda's gaze. "You're still offering the cookies?" I held up my hands, imploring. "Why?"

"People expect them," she answered. "You can't have a Chinese restaurant without the cookies."

I reached out to pluck one from the tray. My fingers closed around the cellophane, and across the table, Linda said, her voice catching, "I wouldn't."

I ripped the paper off, my heartrate speeding up. It's not every day that opening a cookie makes you nervous. My better judgment agreed with Linda—don't open the cookie. Some futures aren't meant to be known.

But I had to know. I had to see for myself what the cookies held in store for me.

I broke the cookie into two pieces, revealing a slip of familiar white paper. I pulled the fortune free and, my breath held, read my destiny.

"A friend is a present you give yourself."

"In bed," Lust added, reading over my shoulder. "You have to add 'in bed' to any fortune."

Small relief flooded through me, and I placed the fortune on the table. "Just to cover all our bases, we should probably talk to your staff," I said to the Wongs. They might have heard or seen something. Unless that's a problem."

Linda shooed this away. "Of course not. I'll make sure you get the contact information for anyone you need. Is there anything else?"

I glanced at Lust, but she was already going to town on her noodles. I turned to Linda. "If we think of something else, we'll be in touch."

seven

. . .

After we finished lunch, I headed out to the street where I called Helen Park. It was a quick conversation. The woman cursed me out, called me a spineless mongrel, spit when she said Linda Wong's name, and then agreed to meet with us the next day. Afterward, I made a half dozen other phone calls to the staff, but no one answered, so I left voicemails.

"I'm not sure what else we should do today." I shoved my phone into my pocket and mopped beads of sweat from my brow. The day was warm, and I was overdressed. "Should we head back to the house? Or should we, I don't know, go get ice cream or something?"

I didn't want any ice cream, but Tricia made it clear we were supposed to entertain our viewers. That included going on fun, cute outings. Going for ice cream was about the cutest, funnest thing my brain could conjure up.

Lust didn't answer, and for a minute, I thought she

hadn't heard me. But when I peered into her face, I saw something was wrong. Lust looked the way Shayda sometimes looked when she watched Hallmark movies or talked to her family in Iran. "Hey. Are you okay?"

Lust swept her fingertips across her cheek, and only then did I realize she was crying. Her face wasn't red or splotchy, which is why I hadn't noticed. Shayda's face always turned colors when she wept. She was what some people might call an ugly crier, though I wouldn't say that. To me, everything Shayda did was beautiful.

"It's fine. I'm fine," Lust lied. "I'm just being silly."

"Emotions are silly," I agreed, "but you're supposed to acknowledge them. At least, that's what my therapist says."

Lust chuckled. "Oh yeah? My therapist says something similar. No, really, it's nothing. It's just…sometimes seeing happy families makes me weepy."

I glanced over my shoulder toward the restaurant. I didn't get the impression that the Wongs were a particularly happy family, but what did I know? "I see. Any reason? Do you not get along with your family?"

Lust looked like she would answer but then shut her mouth, a curious expression taking over her face that I couldn't read. "Actually, let's change the subject. Why don't you tell me about you? Where's your family from?"

This was a line of conversation I really didn't want to have, but if it prevented an episode of crying, I'd embrace it enthusiastically. "I don't know," I said, wavering. "It's kind of a weird story."

Lust rubbed her palms together as if to warm them,

her previous melancholy quickly evaporating. "Ooh, now *that* sounds interesting. Do tell."

We started walking, though we weren't heading toward the car. We were just sort of ambling along, soaking up the sunshine, the wind blowing through our hair. "Well, I'm an orphan. I don't know who my family was because they all disappeared."

Lust's eyes went wide. "Disappeared?"

I nodded. "Yeah. It's…kind of a famous story. You ever heard of the Lovelace Commune out in Santa Barbara?"

Lust shook her head. "I'm from Ohio."

I was pretty sure they had Netflix and libraries even in Ohio, but I let it go. "Oh. Well, the commune was kind of infamous, even before it disappeared. It was an artist's colony started by this guy Sam Lovelace. He was a religious fanatic who believed Jesus was an alien and that the lost books of the Bible taught psychic powers like telekinesis and co-location. He believed deep artistic expression could unlock psychic powers in the mind, so he started this commune."

"I believe that, too," Lust said. "I mean, I don't know about the aliens and stuff. But I do believe deep artistic expression can unlock your inner power."

"Anyway," I continued, "this journalist went out there to do some interviews for a story she was writing. But when she arrived, the entire place was empty. People's cars were still there. The houses were furnished, and closets were filled with clothes. But all the people were gone. The journalist, Anne Lovett, said it was the strangest thing she'd ever seen. Most of the houses were unlocked, so she'd gone inside a few, trying to find some-one. Anyone. It was lunchtime when she arrived, and many of the dining rooms were set with plates and untouched food and everything. She said it was like people were there one second, and in the next second, they vanished. She was dialing the sheriff's department for help when she heard a baby crying."

Without warning, Lust reached over and linked her arm in mine. At her touch, an image flashed through my mind—a woman wearing an elaborate, cream-colored saree with jewels in her hair, a man in an officer's uniform. But just as quickly as they'd come on, the images subsided. "Was that baby you?"

I nodded. "Anne Lovett ran into my house and found me in my cradle. I was the only person she found in the commune, alive or otherwise. The sheriff's department investigated, but none of the other commune members were ever found. Not even their bodies. There was no evidence of foul play or anything like that. One minute, it was a bustling community filled with people, and the next, it was a ghost town. Empty except for me."

Lust whistled and squeezed my upper arm. "My God. It's your very own Lost Colony of Roanoke story, isn't it?"

I had no idea what she was talking about, but I wasn't about to tell her that. Instead, I shrugged. "Yeah, I guess so. There's been lots of books written about it. There was even a popular documentary a few years ago. They wanted to interview me, but I wasn't interested. Never really wanted that kind of notoriety."

Lust glanced surreptitiously at the cameras following us. "Kind of a weird situation for you to be in, then, isn't it, Freak Show?"

I looked down at the sidewalk, trying to hide my face. Something about the way she said *Freak Show* felt intimate, which freaked me out, but not in a bad way, and the fact that I kind of liked it *also* freaked me out. "I didn't have a lot of choice," I said.

Lust purred knowingly. "Yeah. When Tricia gave me that line about fulfilling my deepest desire, I was hooked, too. I'd do *anything* to win this thing. I mean it." There was a fierceness about her when she said this, a tension in how she held her shoulders. "But I guess most people would do just about anything to get what their heart really wants, huh?"

I couldn't answer that, though, so again, I shrugged. "I guess, but that's not me. I mean, I'm not here to win some stupid wish."

Lust cocked her head to the side. "You're lying."

I opened my mouth to say I wasn't, but then I reconsidered. Maybe there *was* a part of me that was here to win my heart's deepest desire. But I wasn't going to be contradicted on camera, so I said, "I'm not lying."

"So then why are you here?"

"I had nowhere else to go after my girlfriend dumped me. I needed a place to stay. Tricia was offering, and no one else was. So that's why I'm here. It's as simple as that."

Lust squeezed my arm again and pressed her body closer to mine. "So what you're saying is, you're single?"

I couldn't help it. I blushed.

———

When we arrived back at the house, someone was screaming.

I pushed Lust aside and flew up the stairs, taking them two at a time, following the screams. Without thinking, I threw open the door to one of the bedrooms and immediately wished I hadn't.

The room was a disaster. Pigsty hardly began to describe it. In addition to the clothes piled in heaps across the room, the trashcan overflowed with tissues and junk food wrappers. The bed was unmade, with a tangle of stained sheets lodged at the base of the foot-board. A bare mattress was covered in books, makeup brushes, and decks of tarot cards. Empty beer bottles, discarded jewelry, and wire hangers added a bit of sparkle to the rest of the detritus.

Amid all of it was Sloth, standing in the center of the room, her hands buried in her hair, fully clothed and dripping wet. She was wailing at the top of her lungs.

"Sloth?" I stepped over a pair of muddy shoes as I approached her. "Are you okay? What's wrong?"

Instead of answering, however, Sloth squeezed her eyes shut, shaking her head wildly from side to side. *"I need everybody to stop thinking about me!"* she screeched. Her whole body was trembling, and I couldn't tell if it was because she was cold and wet or because she was having an episode. I took another step toward her, but before I reached her, I stopped in my tracks.

Something—some kind of translucent, undulating creature—was hovering at the side of the room. Water dripped from slender, human-like limbs, and long hair floated around its head like the being was underwater. As I watched in disbelief, the being evaporated, only to reappear on the other side of the room where it began to nonchalantly shower Sloth's belongings with water.

"Stop that!" Sloth squealed, angry tears streaming down her cheeks. "You're *ruining* my things! Why are you even doing this? Why is this happening?"

I didn't have an answer to that. I was still staring at the impossible existence of this miraculous water creature when someone else burst into the room.

It was Envy. Her skin was blanched, her eyes wide and red-rimmed. She, too, looked as though she'd been crying. A cameraman stood behind her, a blinking camera perched on his shoulder.

"I don't know what to do!" Envy was trembling as she looked around the room. The creature had floated to a new area, dousing everything it found in water. "The undine was supposed to help, but it's making everything *worse!*"

Well, that was an understatement. The books were ruined. The clothes were fine—in fact, they looked like they needed a good wash—but the papers, tarot cards, electronics, and other things that didn't interact well with water, well, they were long past saving.

Envy stomped a foot and thrust out her arm, pointing in the water creature's direction. "Undine! Stop that! Stop *that right now!* Dissolve! Get out of here!" She turned to me, eyes pleading. "I don't know how to command these things. Sometimes they just get out of control."

My jaw dropped as I waved about, indicating the soggy mess all around us. "You did this? You summoned this creature?"

Envy tilted her head back, wrapping her hands around the back of her neck. "*Summoned* is a strong word. I just thought that if we had some help around here, you know, to keep Sloth in line? You know, to balance out her mess? I just thought it would be nice for everybody. It's fine to live in a house with somebody with cleanliness issues, but that means someone else has to take up the slack. I figured I could do that. So I just sort of thought that an undine might be able to fix the situation. But now I can't get her to stop!"

As if on cue, the undine disappeared and reappeared again, soaking a stack of laundry that lined the far wall. I sighed, taking a careful step toward Sloth, who had stopped screaming but was still crying and shaking. "Let's get you out of here," I said, gently placing an arm around her shoulder. But as soon as I touched her, intense images flashed behind my eyes, their accompanying emotions shuddering through my body. Greed scowling at her from across the living room. Wrath sneering, shouldering past her in the hallway. Lust seeing her approaching and going the other way. I saw people I didn't recognize ridiculing and mocking her, their disgust etched all over their faces. I felt their name-calling like so many daggers in my gut: Pig. Deadbeat. Repulsive. Worthless.

My instinct was to pull away, to break the connection that allowed me to see her memories and feel her pain. But if I withdrew, she would think it was her. She would think I was just like all the other people who treated her like she was less than human. But I wasn't like that, and I didn't want her to think I was. So I held on.

As my grip tightened around her, Sloth's crying ceased, her face upturned to mine. Her eyes were wide and round, her lips parting as she exhaled, "Really? You care what I think about you?"

I balked, blinking in surprise. "I—huh? Wait. How did you know…?"

She offered me a tentative smile. "I read minds. I try not to," she explained hurriedly. "But sometimes I can't tune it out. Especially when I'm upset. And right now, I'm *very* upset!" She shot an accusing glance at the undine that was still floating around the room, drenching her things in water. "I'll try very hard not to read your mind, Pride. But do you think you could stay with me awhile? Until I calm down?"

"Sure," I said, guiding her around a growing puddle in the middle of her room. "Let's go downstairs. Envy?"

Envy startled, looking up. "Yeah?"

I sighed and lifted my chin toward the undine. "Please have that fixed by the time we get back."

She nodded vigorously, chewing on her lips. "I will. I promise. I mean, I'll try."

I ushered Sloth downstairs where she settled into the couch, feet tucked beneath her as I hurried to the kitchen to pour her a glass of water. "You need anything else?" I called.

"No," she called back. Her voice sounded calmer. "Thank you."

I returned with the water, which she accepted gratefully. "I'm sorry to be such a nuisance. It's just…that *thing* burst into my room and started spraying water all over my stuff." She sniffled and wiped away the snot that leaked from her nose. "The *nerve* of Envy to sic one of her elementals on me! Who does she think she is? She didn't even *ask*. She just *assumed* I'd want that thing in my room."

I grunted as I settled into the couch beside Sloth. "To be fair, I don't think Envy really thought it through at all. I think she really believed she was doing the house a favor."

But Sloth wasn't listening. "People think because I'm messy, I don't care about my things. But I actually care very much. It's just that so much goes on in my head all the time. I don't have the energy to worry about my physical space. I'm constantly trying to arrange things in my *head*. Especially other people's things." She looked down at her hands, her head shaking as her chin wobbled. "Being a mind reader isn't all it's cracked up to be, you know? People think such awful things all the time. Not just about me. But about each other. And especially about themselves."

I didn't know what to say to that, so I changed the subject. "How did your task go today? You're with Envy and Gluttony, right?"

Sloth nodded as she took another sip of water. "Yeah. It was fine, I guess. Our task is to help this old lady find her son." She rolled her eyes and set the glass on the table. "She swears he's missing because she hasn't heard from him in a week or so, but the police say she does this all the time. She reports him missing, but then he shows up like nothing happened. Apparently, the old woman is kinda…" She whirled her index finger around her temple and made a cuckoo sound. "It seems like a dumb task to me."

I settled into the cushions, crossed my legs, and folded my arms over my chest. "Why does it sound dumb? Even if he's not really missing, imagine the peace of mind you're giving her. Sounds like she needs the help. Anyway, it has to be better than helping a Chinese restaurant figure out who's been meddling with their fortune cookies."

Sloth's cheeks turned pink as she choked down a laugh. "You have to help a Chinese restaurant with a cookie problem? Yeah, that's…Okay, I feel less bad about mine. Hold that thought, though. We'll get back to that. Anyway, I see what you're saying about old Mrs. Romanowsky, but it's *impossible*. She wants us to walk around town and ask people. 'Have you seen this man?'" She dug her phone out of a pocket, tapped something in, and showed me a photo. I leaned in, squinting to get a better look. The photo showed a middle-aged man dressed in a camouflage hunting outfit. A vest was strapped over his chest, sporting various tools and accoutrements attached with velcro. I could barely make out his face.

"*This* is the picture she gave you?" I asked. "Does she think he walks around dressed like this all the time?"

Sloth snorted. "I told you. She's not all there. Luckily, we got a better photo from the police, though they also told us we were wasting our time." Sloth sighed and rubbed her forehead with the heel of her hand as she slipped her phone back into her pocket. "You see what I mean? It's just a lot."

It did sound like a lot. "Do Gluttony and Envy have any ideas?"

Sloth sucked her teeth, her expression melting into something like annoyance. "We didn't get a lot done, to be honest. Envy just walked around the house admiring everything and complaining that this woman's house was so much more pleasant than her own. Gluttony made a beeline for the kitchen to make snacks for everyone. To be fair, he whipped up a *great* pasta dish. But with Gluttony in the kitchen and Envy giving herself a private tour, that left me to deal with the old lady alone. She showed me stuff she collects—stamps and plates and stuff." Sloth wrinkled her nose and threw a glance up to the ceiling, where we heard shuffling and the occasional curse in Envy's voice. She cringed. "I hate to say this only one day in, but as a trio, I'm not sure we're working out."

"The good news is, you'll have a new team eventually," I said.

Sloth waved this away. "I guess. Okay, your turn. Tell me about this fortune cookie situation."

I gave her the short version of the story, and when I was done, she was utterly enthralled. She had stopped crying, which was good, and she even seemed to have forgotten about the undine destroying her bedroom. "So what does your gut say? Do you think it's the Korean lady?"

I scratched my chin, dithering. "Not sure. It's too

early to say. We have to investigate all leads, of course. But the Korean lady angle just seems too obvious, you know?"

"Maybe," Sloth drawled, her voice heavy with uncertainty, "but this isn't a detective movie, Pride. It's real life. Sometimes the obvious answer is the answer."

I opened my mouth to object but then quickly snapped it shut. She was right. This wasn't a scripted assignment from the network. This was a real problem affecting a real family. The Wongs were genuinely and rightfully upset, losing much-needed money, and needed Lust and me to help them. I groaned with chagrin as the realization dawned. "Wow. I'm an idiot. I've been approaching this all wrong."

Sloth leaned forward. "What do you mean?"

"In my regular life, I'm a paranormal investigator," I said. "It's not as glamorous as it sounds. I consult with the police department on special cases. Murders and missing persons, mostly. I see things when I touch people, and I run into more than my fair share of ghosts. I solved a recent case by interviewing a ghost that was the only eyewitness to a murder. So if this were a case, I'd be working from a list of suspects the cops gave me, but I'd also be thinking about who can do something like this."

Sloth nodded. "Right. You mean like the people who had access to the fortune cookies or whatever?"

"No. See, the weird thing about this case is that the fortunes only appeared to the person the fortune was about. Anyone else who read the fortune just saw some innocuous message. That's why the Wongs had a hard time believing the accusations at first. But when their daughter's boyfriend confided that he'd also gotten a dark message and then it came true, that's when they believed. So that makes me wonder."

"Wonder what?"

I drew in a sharp breath. "Who can make people see things that aren't there? A random cook or server or somebody couldn't do this because the *cookies* aren't the problem. There's something else at work here. Something more ominous."

"Like magic?" Sloth breathed.

"*Mind* magic," I agreed. "Thanks, Sloth. You just gave me my first solid lead."

eight

. . .

My personal cameraman followed me as I went upstairs to find Lust. Her door was open, and she was lying in bed reading a book. When she saw me, she set the book aside. "Didn't think I'd see you again so soon. You come to keep me company?" She patted the space beside her on the bed.

I ignored that and jammed my thumb over my shoulder. "Get up. I need you to come with me. I have an idea."

Lust frowned but pulled herself out of bed and slipped her feet into a pair of shoes. "Where are we going? An idea about what? I thought we were done for the day."

I nodded, rubbing my palms together. I was getting excited. They say the best way to get over someone is to get under someone else. But the next best way was to get busy with work. "Yeah, we were, but then I was talking to Sloth, and she gave me a great idea."

Lust's eyebrows shot high on her face. "*Sloth* gave

you an idea? That's interesting. I wouldn't have thought that girl had an original thought to call her own."

I felt my expression darken as my eyes narrowed. "Why would you think something like that? Because she's sloppy? That doesn't make her stupid. And second, I don't know if you know this, but she's a mind reader. So she probably heard you think that."

Strictly speaking, I didn't know if that was true. I had no idea how far Sloth's abilities extended, but I made my point. Lust's cheeks blushed crimson, and she glanced down, avoiding my eyes. "You're right. That was mean. Don't tell her I said anything, would you?"

I grunted. "Assuming she didn't hear you herself, maybe the network will edit it out before they air this episode."

Once outside, Lust and I climbed into the front seats of our car. Our camera crew crowded into the back while I fiddled with the Go-Pro on the dashboard. We were supposed to have it on any time we used the car. "So you never told me where we're headed," Lust said.

"I worked a case a few years ago where people were receiving threatening emails requesting big sums of money. Lots of victims from all over the county. But when our forensic computer guys looked into it, nobody could find these emails. They weren't in the inboxes of the victims, and they hadn't been trashed or archived. They simply didn't exist, even though the victims swore up and down they'd received these emails demanding payment."

"Did the people pay?"

I whistled. "They sure did. Some of them forked

over thousands of dollars out of fear of retribution or a secret getting leaked."

Lust clucked her tongue. "Lots of husbands afraid of their wives finding out about their mistresses, I bet."

"You got it," I agreed. "Well, at the same time I was working that case, I was…seeing someone."

Lust hrmmed. "That girlfriend you're trying to win back?"

I grunted, shaking my head. "No, that's not what I mean. I was actually seeing someone. She was showing up a lot at that time. This…girl. A ghost girl." I cleared my throat and waited for a snide jab, but surprisingly, it never came. I plundered on. "Anyway, sometimes I forgot other people couldn't see her. One day, I was talking to her at the park, and this homeless guy shouts at me, '*You people say I'm crazy, but you're the one seeing things ain't there!*' And that got me thinking—what if nobody could find the emails because they were never there to begin with? What if the victims just *thought* they saw them?"

"And were you right?"

I nodded. "Turned out, all the victims had gone to see this magic show over in La Jolla. This guy, Jack Dempsey, was a mentalist. You know, an entertainment psychic. But he was also a con man. His show included subliminal suggestions that tricked susceptible people into thinking they were being blackmailed. Which they were. Just not in the way they claimed."

Lust pulled her feet up into the seat, wrapping her arms around her knees. "That's crazy. So they caught the guy? We aren't going to a *prison*, are we?"

"Nah, he got out a while ago."

"Well, that's something." Lust wound a lock of hair around a finger. "Forgive me if this is a dumb question, but what's that got to do with our task?"

"I don't think anybody's been messing with the fortune cookies. I think somebody's been messing with people's minds."

Lust made a thinking sound as she looked out the window. "Oh, I get it. I guess that makes sense. So let me ask you for the third time. Where are we going?"

I grinned. "Andre's Spooktacular Bowling."

———

Andre's Spooktacular was on the opposite side of the county in a run-down strip mall featuring a pawn shop, a Payday loan, two lingerie shops, and a laundromat. As we climbed out of the car, Lust looked around, hands dug into her hip pockets. "Reminds me of home," she said, nose wrinkled. "I didn't come all the way to California to spend time in a place like this."

"Even California has poor parts of town," I chided her. "But I take your point. This place looks like where Hollywood dreams go to die."

It was the middle of the day, and Andre's was mostly empty. The smell of decades-old cigarette smoke and stale beer hung in the air, and the soles of our shoes stuck to the moldy carpet as we walked. Lust made a disgusted sound in her throat, and though I didn't acknowledge it, I agreed with her sentiment. Andre's had seen better days.

"I guess I can see why they call this place Andre's Spooktacular." She glanced around at the stained walls, the grimy tables and chairs, the paint peeling off the ceiling. "It's absolutely terrifying."

"You think so?" I indicated the dollar store Halloween decor someone had halfheartedly displayed. Ancient plastic skeletons yellowed with age hung from the ceiling, covered in dust and cobwebs. Cheesecloth ghosts haunted the corners, lopsided and decayed. The muffled sounds of a moaning ghost and rattling chains fluttered in from overhead speakers that crackled due to faulty wiring. It somewhat marred the effect. "Seems cheesy to me."

Lust stared at me with an unreadable expression. "Right. Super literal. I forgot." She patted me on the arm. "I like you, Freak Show. You're not like anyone else."

I didn't know how I was supposed to take that, so I let the conversation drop and headed to the check-in counter. The girl working the desk didn't look up from her phone. "You guys here to bowl a game?"

I shook my head. "Here to see Jack Dempsey. He in?"

The girl looked up then, her face slack. She wasn't really a girl, though. Now that I could see her face, she was older than her cotton candy pigtails and blue eyeshadow led me to believe. She looked like a middle-aged woman who called in some heavy favors to get cast as a teenaged girl in a terrible horror film. "Who's asking?"

I hesitated, thinking of the cameras and Tricia

Woodward's adamant direction not to use our real names during filming. But I couldn't exactly go around to old acquaintances calling myself Pride. I'd never hear the end of it. "Sid Sheridan," I said finally. The network could edit out my real name if they wanted. "And tell him I'm in a hurry."

The 40-year-old teenager snapped her gum and threw me one last skeptical glance before picking up the phone—an actual landline—and pressing a button. "Jack? Someone's here to see you. Sid Sheridan? Says it's urgent." A pause, then a nod. "You got it."

She hung up the phone and tilted her head in a vague direction. "He's in the back."

I thanked her, and we made our way in the general direction she'd jerked her head. I had no idea what 'in the back' meant—he could have been in the parking lot or the john for all I knew. But it didn't take long to find him. He was sitting alone in a dusty room behind a desk covered in papers and empty soft drink cans. He looked just like I remembered. Tall and balding with a potbelly and a nose too large for his face, Jack Dempsey didn't so much as give me a second glance when we walked in. He only had eyes for Lust. He leaped to his feet, a smarmy smile on oily lips as he admired the view. "Well, now, it's not every day a beautiful woman comes asking for me. I should play the lotto or something, eh? Gotta be my lucky day."

Lust walked up to him, all confidence and steel, and with a voice that could have frozen the devil's spit, said, "Hey buddy. My eyes are up here."

Dempsey recoiled, his lecherous grin morphing into

a sneer. "Feminazi type, eh? Shoulda known. Equal rights this, I'm not a piece of meat that. Bet you change your tune when the bill for dinner comes, though, right?"

Lust didn't miss a beat. "I promise you will *never* find out."

As gently as I could, I nudged Lust aside, interrupting before things got nasty. Dempsey was a pig, but we needed his help. "Hey, knock it off, okay? We're not here to pick a fight. We're working on a case."

Dempsey tumbled into his chair, brushing aside a mound of papers as he kicked his feet up to the desk. "Bully for you, Sheridan. You don't actually think I'm gonna *talk* to you, do ya? I served time on account of you. Penitentiary time."

"You served time for committing a *crime*," I reminded him. "I had nothing to do with it. Come on, Dempsey. Be the bigger man. Think of it this way—I'll owe you."

"You already owe me," he growled. "That's the point, Sheridan. That's what I'm saying. You're in a hole so deep, you couldn't dig your way out."

That was a ridiculous thing to say because the depth of the hole had nothing to do with whether further digging would get you out. It really depended on the nature of the hole and the tools at hand, but that wasn't the point, so I let it slide. "Dempsey—"

But before I could make my pitch, Lust sauntered around to the other side of the desk and planted her butt on the edge. For all that he'd dismissed her as a feminazi a few moments ago, Dempsey couldn't take his eyes off her now. She leaned in, lowered her voice, and said, "You're gonna help us with this case, Jack Dempsey. And you don't want anything in return. You just want to help."

Dempsey's jaw went slack as his eyes glazed over, a blank expression replacing his earlier sneer. His whole body relaxed, and he blinked lazily until whatever cloud had settled over him dissipated. He sat up, loudly clearing the phlegm from his throat. "I'm feeling generous today, Sheridan. Must be your lucky day. How can I help?"

Lust looked over her shoulder and dropped me a wink before walking back around the desk, coming to stand at my side. I gave her a questioning look, but when all she did was shrug in response, I dove in. "Let's say you wanted to make people read something ominous in their fortune cookie messages. How would you go about doing that?"

Dempsey narrowed his eyes at me. "I heard you got canned at the county. What's this about?"

I shot a quick glance toward the cameras. "Private customer," I said. "Pay's not great, but." I shrugged and offered an awkward smile. Guys like Dempsey liked it when you admitted things weren't going so hot. Made them feel big.

Dempsey grunted. "Private customer. Right. And this is the case? Fortune cookies?"

My face grew hot at the scorn I noted in his voice, and before I could reel in my ego, I said, "You're assistant managing a run-down bowling alley, Dempsey.

Your mother's not exactly boasting about you to the ladies at Bridge club."

Lust elbowed me in the side, throwing me a reproving glance. She was right; insulting him wasn't going to get me any information. The first rule of interrogation was to butter up the other party. Wheedling and flattery weren't exactly my forte, but at least I didn't have to tick him off. I tried again. "Look, I didn't come here to bust your balls. Just answer the question."

Dempsey glowered at me, lips pinched as he stroked his chin and clucked his tongue. I waited, but with each second that passed, the more confident I became that I'd overstepped. Dempsey wasn't gonna talk. I was thinking of something to say to put him back in the driver's seat when he sighed and threw his hands up. "Whatever. Look, there are two ways to go about this: blanket the whole venue in suggestion, or go after individual people. For the venue approach, you have to get the crowd susceptible first—get them in a hypnotic state. Several ways to do that: music, smell, even certain lighting. But like I said, it doesn't always work. People are talking, flirting, drinking—they're not necessarily tuned in to their environment. Anyway, you still gotta plant the suggestion in the ones you managed to influence. Best and easiest way to do that is to encode it into music. It isn't hard. Anyway, the suggestion always has a trigger—in your case, reading a fortune cookie. They read the cookie and BAM! They think they read a message that wasn't there."

I nodded. "Okay. How popular is this tactic?"

"Very. It's what most good con artists—including

yours truly—go for. Less chance of getting caught. Plus, the bigger the area of effect, the more marks available. But it's hit-or-miss. You can't guide it, can't tailor it to any specific person, you see what I'm saying? It's generic."

I said, "Right. Okay. Let's say that's my guy—Joe Schmoe Con Man using suggestion. Gimme a profile. What kind of person am I looking for?"

Dempsey folded his arms across his chest and blew out a puff of air. "Pretty much anybody with basic brainwave training and a decent audio editing program could do it."

"And where do you get brainwave training?"

Dempsey snorted. "These days? YouTube."

That wasn't the answer I'd hoped for, and my increasing optimism took a hard left. But then Lust said, "Well, but the person responsible would need access to the restaurant, right? To cause the hypnotic state in the first place? And then to play the track with the suggestion?"

Dempsey nodded. "Oh, sure. Once the marks leave the venue, they're not susceptible anymore. They wake up."

Lust looked at me with wide eyes. "In that case, it has to be one of the staff," she said. "Or at least someone with access to the sound system."

"Not necessarily." Dempsey held up two fingers. "Your suspect could have used method number two—up close and personal. It's way more difficult but more effective. You can even plant a suggestion in advance and set it to go off at a certain time and place—like, say, when the mark reads a cookie at a certain restaurant." He couldn't keep the ridicule from his voice as he said this. Honestly, I couldn't really blame him.

"And for the up close and personal kind, anybody could do that, too, right? Anybody with access to the marks?"

"Anybody with the right talent," Dempsey corrected. "And there's not a lot of those folks running around."

Now we were getting somewhere. "What do you mean?"

Dempsey twitched his over-large nose and rearranged his feet on the desk. "People always think the large-scale tricks are the hardest, but it's actually the up close and personal stuff that's the doozy. Think about it this way. When you've got a whole audience in front of you, there's a million ways to distract their attention from what you're trying to pull. You got sparkly lights, amazing sounds, a hot woman on stage." He glanced at Lust and winked when he said this. "But when it's up close and personal, that person's attention is a hundred percent on you. You got to be at the top of your game to get what you want from them. I always admired the guys who could pickpocket. Distract you while they touched your body, removing jewelry and watches and stuff? Man, what a gift."

I ignored the wrongness of referring to swindlers and cheats as having a gift. "So what kind of person can do the up close and personal attack? Can you learn that from YouTube?"

Dempsey waved that away. "Nah. Those folks aren't manipulating music tracks. They do it with their voice.

Or a look. Maybe the way they smell—hell, I don't know. It's not something you can learn—you're born with it. Kinda like you and your ghosts."

For some reason, that made my skin crawl. Goosebumps broke out over my skin, and I grimaced, unreasonably insulted. "I'm not a con artist," I said.

"Never said you were. Just meant maybe she's born with it, maybe it's Maybelline." Dempsey removed his feet from the desk and stood, stretching his arms over his head and arching his back. The buttons at the belly of his shirt strained. "Are we done here?"

I glanced at Lust. "You have any more questions?"

She shook her head. "No, I'm good."

I returned my attention to the con man. "Thanks, Dempsey. You were a big help, whether you wanted to be or not."

He scratched his nose with one hand and made a rude gesture with the other.

We took that as our cue to leave.

———

"Okay, so we know the mechanism for how this is happening. Or at least we have some leads. But I'm still not sure how to figure out the bigger question."

Lust cocked an eyebrow at me as we climbed into the car. "And what's that?"

"The victims in this case didn't just read an ominous message. They read an ominous message that also came true. That's the part I'm struggling with. Even con men like Dempsey can't predict the future. So whoever implanted those suggestions is not only an accomplished mentalist, they're also some kind of fortuneteller. And that's the part I just can't wrap my brain around."

I started up the car, and we drove in silence for a while, my mind combing over the facts of the case. As I was replaying the meeting with Dempsey in my mind, however, an unnerving feeling crawled up my spine.

"Hey, Lust? Can I ask you something?"

She shrugged. "Sure."

"How did you do that thing with Dempsey back there?"

She hesitated, winding a lock of hair around a finger. "What do you mean?"

My grip tightened on the wheel. "He wasn't going to talk. Dempsey doesn't exactly hate me, but we're not buddies, either. I was prepared to butter him up good, but I didn't have to. You just walked over there and turned on your charm, and suddenly, it was like he was a zombie. Or hypnotized." I paused to let the effect of my words sink in. "So, what did you do back there?"

Silence engulfed the car. The only things I heard were the noise from the highway and the cameramen in the backseat squirming, trying to get comfortable. But finally, Lust answered, her voice softer than usual. "I'm a siren."

I snapped my head around. "A what?"

"It's my psychic ability. It's why the network cast me on the show. That and these personality flaws." She grabbed her breasts as she said this, and from the corner of my eye, I saw the color crawl up her cheeks. "I can get people to do things. Not any person, of course. But certain people. I use my voice to…*seduce* them into giving me what I want. I don't even really know how I do it. Not really. I just decide to convince someone to do something, and they do it."

"I see." I wanted to leave it at that because part of me really didn't want to hear more. But the rest of me was too curious for my own good, so I asked, "So, what're the criteria for someone being susceptible to your charms?"

Again, she paused. "Well." She looked down, fidgeting with the strings that hung from her cut-off shorts. "They have to be into women."

I felt my cheeks flush red as beads of sweat popped out on my brow. "So it would work on me, then?"

Lust shrugged. "I guess so, yeah. If you like women."

The energy in the car shifted as the full meaning of Lust's words registered. Even the cameramen made subtle disapproving sounds at her revelation. I was suddenly anxious, my mouth going dry while my palms began to sweat. I felt like a rabbit who just smelled a nearby wolf, and I swallowed down the instinct to get as far away from Lust as possible. She must have felt my growing discomfort, too, because she sighed and shrank away from me, drawing herself closer to the car door. "Now you think I'm a manipulative sociopath," she said.

I shot her a sideways glance. She didn't look like a wolf. Maybe that made it worse. "I don't know exactly what I think. I *am* worried that you're dangerous."

My words hung in the air, stark and naked and true. I *did* think someone like that was dangerous. But I also didn't want to hurt Lust's feelings because I needed her to help out with our case. So I said, "I guess I don't like the idea of someone planting ideas in my head. I'm garbage at understanding other people's motivations and emotions, but at least I can control my own, you know?"

"You don't, though." She said this without looking at me. "Nobody does. You've already been conditioned to think a certain way just by being alive in Western society. Advertisers, social media, even your family and friends —everybody puts ideas in your head all the time. Lose weight. Buy name brands. Make more money. Vote Democrat." She ticked these off on her fingers without missing a beat. "Everyone around you has an agenda, even if they don't know it. Even *you* have an agenda."

That last part was definitely true, but my agenda was simple: get Shayda back. It had nothing to do with influencing other people. "That's different," I said. "That's not personal."

"Oh, really?" She angled her body so she was fully facing me. I couldn't look directly at her, but I saw how taut her body was and how her eyes flashed in the sunlight. "Tell me something, Pride. And be honest. When you see a fat person wearing a bikini, what's the *first* thing you think?"

"That maybe they should have worn a one-piece instead." As soon as I said that, however, I felt terrible. A hot flush crept up my neck. "Wait, no. That's an awful thing to say, and I'm not even sure I believe that. Yeah, on second thought, people should wear whatever they want."

"Bingo." Lust pointed a triumphant finger at me. "But that was the *second* thing you thought. Your first thought was conditioned by society. Let that sink in, Freak Show. Your *second thought* was your own. Your *first thought* belonged to someone else."

I wanted to argue, mainly because she'd just proven me wrong, and I hated that, but I *couldn't* argue because she was right, and no amount of arguing would make me less wrong. So instead, I said, "Well, I see your point, but I still don't like the idea of someone else putting ideas in my head."

She turned away from me then, pressing her forehead against the window. "Of course you don't. No one does. You don't have to worry about me, though. I won't try to charm you. I like you. But I can't help that this is the way I am. Not any more than you can help seeing ghosts."

Everything she was saying made sense, but the more sense she made, the more I didn't like it. And sometimes, when I was upset and flustered, I said things I later regretted, which is why I said, "Well, at least this conversation helped me learn more about the person we're looking for."

"It did?"

I nodded. "Yeah. Turns out, we might be looking for a sociopath like you."

nine

. . .

Things were tense between Lust and me after that. We drove the rest of the way in silence, and when we arrived back at the house, she went straight up to her room without greeting the other housemates. She brushed past Envy on the stairs, who gave me a questioning look as she jabbed a thumb over her shoulder.

"What's wrong with Lust?"

I plopped down on the couch, kicking off my shoes as Envy took a seat next to me, still looking puzzled. "Do you know what her ability is?"

"Sure." Envy's puzzlement deepened. "She's a siren. So what?"

I chuckled dryly and made a face. "Let me guess. You're straight."

Envy peered at me for a moment, then folded her arms over her chest. "Oh, I get it," she said. "You're worried she's gonna mind-trick you into doing something you don't want to do." I noted a trace of disapproval in her voice. "That's not how it works, you know."

"Isn't it?"

Envy made a disgusted sound and looked away. "Did you even *ask* her about her talent? Or did you just assume the worst?"

"I assumed the worst," I admitted.

"Well, according to what she told me, she can only override your social conditioning. She can only give you an impulse. If you're a thoughtful person—someone who really considers their actions—your own convictions will kick in, and her suggestion gets thrown out."

"I guess that makes me feel better," I said.

Envy smiled. "Good."

The thing was, though, hearing these words *didn't* make me feel better. I only said that because it seemed like the right thing to say. But the truth was, it made me feel worse. I considered the reasons:

1. I didn't bother to ask Lust more questions about her ability. It was selfish and short-sighted, two things I was supposed to be working on if I wanted to get Shayda back.
2. I wasn't a thoughtful person. I ran on instinct almost all the time. So if Lust wanted to brainwash me, she probably could, and she wouldn't even break a sweat.

"Do you want me to go talk to her?"

I hesitated. "You can go talk to her if you want. I

don't mind. Or you can stay here. I don't mind that, either."

Envy chuckled. "I meant, do you want me to go talk to her on your behalf?"

"Oh." I shook my head. "No, that's okay. Thanks, though."

Envy lingered a moment before rising and reaching out to muss my hair. "Cheer up, okay? I'll see you at dinner."

I wasn't hungry, but according to my contract with the network, I was supposed to attend house meals any time I was home. Apparently, it would be good for ratings. So I went to my room, got cleaned up, and came back down to dinner, which turned out to be a feast.

Gluttony was bustling to and from the kitchen carrying dishes that smelled so good, my mouth watered despite my lack of hunger. The table was already heaped with roast chicken, buttery green beans, fresh-baked dinner rolls, and baked sweet potatoes. I followed Gluttony into the kitchen and gestured around. "Anything I can do?"

"Ancestors help me," he muttered, eyes turned to the ceiling. The utterance was half prayer, half curse. "These fools think I actually want their help." He elbowed me aside with a meaty arm. "No, get on outta here. People always think offering to help in the kitchen is friendly, but you just in my way. Step on out."

Gluttony shooed me out into the dining room, and while he grumbled and complained and carried out more plates, I sat down at the table next to Sloth. She looked happy to see me. "You guys make any progress on your task?" she asked, chewing on the end of a pigtail.

"Some," I said. "You?"

"Not really." She sighed and helped herself to a serving of sweet potatoes. She spilled most of them onto the table. "And tomorrow already doesn't look good, either."

One by one, the rest of the housemates gathered at the table. Everyone had come down except Lust. The table had been set for seven, so the empty seat was conspicuous. Wrath pointed at it with his fork.

"Is anybody gonna go get the nympho?"

A few snickers went around the table, but they died out when Envy snapped, "Stop it." She gave Wrath a withering stare. "She has a name."

Wrath snorted. "Calling her Lust is better than Nympho?"

Envy opened her mouth to retort but shut it again, looking down into her lap.

"She'll come down when she's ready," Gluttony said. "I'm not about to let this food get cold, not after I been in the kitchen all afternoon. Let's eat."

Greed dug into the green beans with a vengeance. "This is phenomenal," he said. "I mean, really great. If anybody's not going to eat theirs, let me know. I mean, just fantastic."

"Better be after all the work I put in," Gluttony said with a grin. "I wanted this dinner together to be special, so I added a little something extra."

I glanced up from my still-empty plate. "What kind of something extra?"

Gluttony winked. "Eat it and find out."

After the earlier debacle with Lust, I wasn't so sure I wanted to deal with any more surprises. Still, I also didn't want to appear ungrateful, so I took small samplings of everything. I took one bite of the roasted chicken, and then another, and then another. And as I ate, my muscles relaxed, my mood lifted, and my appetite ignited in a blaze of glory. I was just about to go in for seconds when I realized what was going on.

"You're a kitchen witch!" I exclaimed, delighted by the discovery. I'd never met a kitchen witch before. They aren't as plentiful as social media might have you believe. Just because you can follow a recipe for chocolate chip cookies and you're handy with a camera and lighting doesn't make you a wizard. "This is incredible. Like, wow, Gluttony. You're really talented."

The big man huffed. "I know it." He gestured toward the green beans. "Those are my specialty. They make you gabby. I don't like silence. Secrets live in silence. Green beans'll make you the life of the party."

Everyone went for the green beans at once.

As we ate, tensions melted away, and laughter flowed. We shared the highlights of our days and traded questions back and forth. After a while, it was like we'd known each other for years, which was precisely the point. Gluttony's magic was the most fun I'd had in a long while.

But as good as dinner made me feel, I couldn't stop thinking about Lust.

Later that night, as I was climbing into bed and preparing a mental checklist of tomorrow's activities, I heard a familiar voice in the dark.

"Boy, did you ever mess up today."

I squeezed my eyes shut and rolled onto my side, giving the specter my back. "Now's not a good time," I said.

The ghost girl snorted, and I sensed her rolling her eyes at the back of my head. "You always say that. It's never a good time with you. But you messed up this time. So you need to fix it."

"I can't," I said into the darkness. "I know I messed up. But it's not something I can fix."

I heard the shuffling of spectral feet coming around to my side of the bed. I didn't open my eyes, but I sensed the ghost hovering near my face. "Apologize," she said.

I pretended to be asleep, but the ghost didn't move. "I know you're awake," she said. "Nobody falls asleep that fast. Even goldfish need 30 seconds to fall asleep."

Exasperated, I opened my eyes. The ghost's face was mere inches from mine. Her eyes were wide and round in the dark, the corners of her mouth turning down into a frown. I never would've thought a child could look so disappointed in someone. I rolled over onto my other side. "I can't apologize, so don't ask."

The ghost sucked her teeth. "You're such a jerk."

I pulled the blankets up over my head, hoping to muffle the sound of her voice. But I heard her perfectly when she said, "You can't just go around hurting other people because *you* feel uncomfortable or because *you* don't understand what the big deal is. Maybe Shayda's sister's wedding wasn't a big deal to you, but it was a big deal to her. You made a promise."

"That was an accident!" I cried. "I know it was a big deal! I screwed up!"

"You *let* yourself mess up. If it really mattered, you would have set reminders. You would have told the detective you couldn't work that day. You would have done *something!* But you didn't because the only person you think about is yourself because you're too *scared* to think about other people. You're supposed to be a grown-up. Grown-ups are supposed to know better."

"Children are supposed to do what they're told," I retorted. "Go away."

"No."

The ghost didn't so much as twitch. I rolled over again to find her still standing there, hands on her hips, head tilted to one side, toes tapping. I kicked off my blankets and sat up. "If I apologize in the morning, will you give me a break? I need to get some sleep. I have a lot to do tomorrow."

The ghost lifted her shoulders, a halfhearted attempt at a shrug. "Depends."

"Depends on what?"

"Depends on how good of an apology you give her. You really hurt her, you know. She didn't deserve that. She didn't do anything except tell you the truth."

Shame lit me up and set my skin on fire. I hated getting admonished by ghosts, especially pint-sized ghosts with boundary issues. I threw myself back into the pillows, flinging my forearm over my eyes, trying to blot the day from my memory and the ghost's words from my ears. But she was right. I messed up, and I had to fix it.

"I promise I'll make this right," I told her. "I promise. Now get out of here. Go."

I didn't see her leave, but after a few moments, I felt alone. And not just alone, but lonely.

I pulled the blankets up under my chin and tucked my knees to my chest. I closed my eyes and tried to breathe low and slow, but I didn't fall asleep for a long, long time.

The next day, Lust and I arrived at our appointment with Helen Park fifteen minutes early. She had agreed to meet us at her house. We parked the car, and as we crossed the street, I reached out, grabbing Lust's wrist. She halted and turned, gently freeing herself from my grasp. Her expression was neutral when she asked, "Can I help you with something?"

It's now or never, I told myself. I sucked in a steadying breath. "About what I said yesterday. I shouldn't have called you a sociopath."

"If that's what you think about me, then I'm glad you said it." She crossed her arms over her chest, shrugging like none of this mattered. But her face didn't match her carefree body language, and that's how I knew she was acting. "I'd rather know where I stand. I would hate to have someone be nice to my face only to slag me behind my back."

I shook my head. "I wouldn't talk bad about you behind your back. I'm not much of a gossip. It's one of my few good qualities."

Lust's eyes flickered toward me, and I saw some of the tension ease from her shoulders. She still didn't say anything, though.

"Look, Lust, we have to work together. I genuinely want to help the Wongs get the restaurant back on its feet. I know you want that, too. Right? You want to win. This will go better if the two of us are on good terms."

Lust stared me down, nostrils flared. "Is that supposed to be an apology? Because I never heard the words 'I'm sorry.'"

I rubbed the nape of my neck, avoiding Lust's gaze. "Come on, Lust. I'm trying here." *Good job*, I thought sullenly. *You're making it all about* you *now. That's the opposite of what you're supposed to do.* If I ever went back to therapy, Dr. Xena would have a field day with this one.

If Lust noticed my inner turmoil, however, she didn't let on. She was winding a lock of hair around her finger as she looked up, eyes blinking quickly. It was a moment before I realized she was trying not to cry. "You really hurt my feelings, Pride. I opened up to you, and you made me feel like a jerk."

I shoved my hands in my pockets and looked down at the ground. "I know."

"I want to help the Wongs, too. And that's the only reason I'm accepting your non-apology. I rarely give people second chances." She took a step toward me and placed two fingers under my chin, lifting my face to meet her gaze. "I promise I'll never use my powers on you," she said. "And I always keep my word."

Before I could say anything else, Lust was already turning away, heading for Helen's house. It wasn't exactly the reconciliation I'd imagined. But it was better than nothing.

ten

. . .

I rang the doorbell, and after a moment, I heard shuffling on the other side of the door followed by a shout of, "Keep playing! And don't rush!"

The door opened to reveal a small, scowling Asian woman with perfectly coiffed hair and not a speck of makeup out of place. She had an ageless face—she could have been anywhere between 30 and 100, but the silver in her hair told me she was older. When she saw us, her scowl deepened, but she opened the door wider, stepping to one side. "Well, don't just stand there. You might as well come in. I'm almost done with my lesson."

Piano music drifted in from another room. Lust and I followed Helen into a living area, where our host gestured impatiently toward the couch. The piano playing continued as Lust and I took our seats. I didn't know anything about the piano, but whoever was playing seemed very talented. I recognized the tune, but I couldn't have named it if you'd paid me. Helen held up a finger as she disappeared into the adjoining room.

The music halted. "No, you're rushing again. Go back to the coda. And this time, play with your emotions. This isn't an act, Ruby. The audience can tell if you're faking it. You have to love each measure, or you might as well get out of here right now."

After a brief silence, the music picked up again, but this time was subtly different. The tempo was slower, more languid. I closed my eyes, imagining the pianist curled over the keys, eyes darting over her score, caressing the ivories as she breathed in time with the music. After a while, the playing stopped, and the house filled with silence. I heard the smile in her voice when Helen Park said, "Much better."

The squeak of the piano bench was accompanied by the thump of a piano lid closing, and a moment later, Helen Park entered the living room, followed by Ruby Wong. Ruby smiled and waved, arranging her hair around her shoulders just like she did the first time we'd met. Today, she was wearing a faded t-shirt that read, "I brake for dolphins." That didn't even make sense, but I guess that was par for the course with teenagers. Their prefrontal cortex wasn't fully developed, and that's why they made such terrible decisions, like spending money on illogical t-shirts. At least, that's what I'd heard.

"Hello again!" Ruby said, coming to stand before Lust and me. She was holding sheet music in both hands. "What are you guys doing here?"

Lust glanced from the girl to the older woman, who was now standing with her arms crossed, her scowl still etched into her brow. "Your parents said we should talk to Mrs. Park. You know. About the disturbances at the restaurant."

Ruby cringed, her mouth falling open. Her nostrils flared, and her cheeks grew hot pink as she cursed under her breath, shaking her head. "They just don't listen," she hissed. "What did they tell you? Did they say Mrs. Park had something to do with our fortune cookie incident? Is that what they said? Did they say she's the only one who would benefit from their misfortune?"

Lust and I exchanged looks. "Something like that," I agreed reluctantly.

Ruby dropped into an armchair, setting her sheet music aside as she leaned forward onto her knees, pointing a finger at us. "I'll tell you what's causing the problem at the restaurant," she said. "It's not Mrs. Park or anybody else in this town. It's the wights."

Now, I sat up taller, wrinkling my brow in confusion. "The wights? You mean the supernatural waiters?"

"Servers," Lust corrected me.

I nodded. "Servers. Right. Them?"

"Yes," Ruby said. "*Wights*. I've been reading a lot about them, and it turns out it's not uncommon for earthbound spirits to drive people crazy. They can get in your psyche and make you believe things. See things. It happens a lot more often than people think. Sometimes, especially in older people, it can look like mental deterioration or senility."

This was new information to me, but then again, I was an expert on ghosts, not non-corporeal, non-human entities. And even calling me a ghost expert was a stretch. "So you're saying the wights are making the customers see things? But your parents have had the wights at the restaurant for years. Why is it just happening now?"

Ruby nodded like she'd been expecting this response. "According to the experts I've been reading, wights grow increasingly vicious over time. The longer they're connected to a place, the more likely they are to do mental damage to those around them. So the wights may be just now becoming powerful enough to harm my parents' patrons." Ruby sighed, settling back into the armchair. "I've tried to explain this to my parents, you know. But they don't listen. They think someone is behind this." She gestured toward her piano instructor. "But Mrs. Park wouldn't do anything to hurt them. I know she wouldn't."

"And I don't have to, anyway," Helen said. She'd been standing this whole time, but now she came to sit next to Lust and me. "My restaurant is doing fine. I do enough business to stay busy, but not so much that I don't have a moment to myself. I enjoy teaching piano. I couldn't do that if I was working all the time at the restaurant. My husband helps, but you know how men are." She tittered as she said this, and Lust and I both smiled even though I was pretty sure only Lust knew what she meant. "So you see, I have no motive. But the Wongs are stubborn people. They want to believe it's me, so they've convinced themselves it's true. And now here you are, asking questions and trying to make me look bad."

Lust waved her hands in front of her face, her mouth falling into a frown. "No, we're not here to make you look bad. We just want answers. We want to help the Wongs get the restaurant back on its feet. I do have a question, though." Lust reached up toward her hair, stroking it absently. "Eric said they've had trouble with you in the past. Do you know what he was referring to?"

Helen huffed and rolled her eyes, pinching her lips together. "Oh, sure, I know what he's talking about. Old news. It was back when they first opened. They were subletting the place from another tenant. That was illegal in Odyssey at the time. I explained to the building owner what was happening because he was my cousin. I was looking out for his interests. That's all it was. I wasn't trying to stop the Wongs from renting the space. I just wanted to make sure that they had a contract with my cousin and not with the previous tenant." She held up her hands questioningly. "Is that so wrong?"

"That seems reasonable," I agreed. "Have you and the Wongs had other beef over the years? Any other reason Linda Wong would be so convinced you're behind all of this?"

Helen glanced toward Ruby, and the girl tilted her head forward, a subtle but unmistakable nod. She was giving Helen permission to say something. The older woman sucked in a breath and twisted her hands in her lap. "I hate to say this because I don't like to start rumors. But I think Linda might be jealous of the relationship I have with Ruby. She's here almost every day, and I spend more one-on-one time with her than her own mother does. That's not a criticism," Helen said, holding up a hand to preempt an objection that wasn't coming. At least, not from me. "It's just a fact. Linda and Eric work hard to keep that restaurant running. That doesn't always leave a lot of time for family. That's a choice that Linda made, but now I think she's regretting it. Ruby is all grown up now and moving out, and her mom realizes what little time they have left. I think she wants to turn her daughter against me so they can have more time together." The older woman lifted her shoulders in a defeated shrug. "I know how women get when their nest goes empty. It happened to me, too. I keep trying to tell Linda it will pass. Over time, she'll find her happiness again. But she doesn't listen. To her, I'm still the enemy."

I'd only been half-listening to this, partly because family dynamics didn't interest me and partly because I'd been distracted by Ruby's t-shirt. I must've been mulling it over subconsciously because the meaning finally struck me, and I snapped my fingers. "Oh, I get it. Like a Sea-Doo."

Ruby blinked. "Huh?"

"Your shirt," I said, smiling. "I've been wondering how you could brake for dolphins since dolphins aren't in the streets. But Sea-Doos have brakes, don't they?"

Ruby glanced down at her shirt, brows knit together, and then looked back up, offering a shrug. "Oh, I don't know. I guess? I've never actually been on a Sea-Doo. That's more of a rich people thing," she explained.

That made sense. "So then what's the deal with the t-shirt?"

Ruby puffed out her chest and grinned. "Oh! Well, I'm super into the animal rights community here in Odyssey. It's important to look out for creatures who can't look out for themselves. After all, fish are friends. Not food." She gave a smug smile as she said this. "I'm also a vegan. Imagine how difficult it is to be working at a Chinese restaurant," she said, her nose scrunched.

Lust murmured her agreement. "I can only imagine. You're such a good daughter for going against your ethics to work for your parents."

Ruby cast a sidelong glance at Helen Park. "Well…I mean, it's not like I have much choice. In my culture, kids are expected to obey their parents. But my parents are really cool," she added hurriedly. "They are. I mean, they let me join ORCA, and they really, *really* didn't want to."

I was ready to let this line of conversation drop because my interest in Ruby's relationship with her parents was low. But Lust leaned forward, her curiosity piqued. "What's ORCA?"

"Odyssey Repertory and Community Artists," Ruby said. "It's the local acting company. They offer classes, workshops, all kinds of stuff. Agents and casting directors from Hollywood come down every so often to scout talent. I don't have enough of a portfolio yet to attract attention," Ruby said, a self-pitying frown marring her expression. "But I'm playing Hermia in our production of *A Midsummer Night's Dream.* Opening night is coming up. You should come!"

I couldn't think of anything less appealing than watching amateur actors butcher Shakespeare, but I smiled anyway. "Thanks, but I'm not really into theater."

"I wasn't either at first," she said. "Stage acting

isn't the same as being in the movies, which is what I really want. But it's helping me become a better actor, and as a result, my YouTube channel has really taken off. It's hard letting it all hang out, though, you know? Hiding emotions is way easier." (I almost snorted. Out of the mouths of babes.) "Especially around here. There's a pretty big difference between the haves and the have-nots, and it pays to look like it doesn't really bother you, even when it does. At my school, especially."

Despite my best intentions to stay aloof, this line of conversation piqued my curiosity. "What do you mean, especially at school?"

"Well, I know it's been a long time since you were in high school, but don't you remember how it was?" I cringed, and Lust nudged me in the side, covering her face to hide her laughter. Ruby didn't seem to notice. She continued, "Cliques and stuff, you know? In our school, it's money that divides us. The rich kids run the school. They run the student council, the athletic teams…everything. Most of them are jerks. They act like because they have money, they can do whatever they want. Unfortunately, here in Odyssey, they're not entirely wrong."

Helen nodded at this. "It's true. From the outside, Odyssey looks like a perfect beach resort town. A nice place to vacation, relax, get some sun. But underneath all that?" She shuddered. "It's just rich people doing what they do best. Lying, cheating, being corrupt. That's why it's ridiculous that Linda and Eric Wong think I'm behind sabotaging their business. People much more influential than me would love to see their restaurant shuttered for good."

Finally, we were getting back on track, uncovering the kind of information we came here for in the first place. "Oh yeah? Like who?"

Helen Park pinched her lips together, huffing noisily. "The city council has been trying to shut down that place for the past six months. It's an eyesore. That building? The haunted house facade? It's contrary to how they want to portray the city. The city has been trying for years to lure Hollywood magnates and other big-name, new-money people down here. And they've been successful. Our real estate prices have shot through the roof, and they weren't reasonable to begin with. Beach town, you know," she said. "Last month, the city council introduced a proposition to prohibit buildings that didn't fit into a beach aesthetic from operating within the city limits. But the voters shot it down, though narrowly."

Lust turned to me, sucking her bottom lip thoughtfully. "The Wongs *did* say the city council was full of racists that wished them harm." She turned back to Helen. "Have *you* had trouble with any of them?"

Helen shook her head. "Not like the Wongs. I don't think the city council is racist. I think they're just capitalists looking for the most profit."

"Mom thinks everyone is racist," Ruby said, rolling her eyes. "Anyway, I need to get going." She climbed to her feet, retrieving her sheet music as she headed toward the front door. "I'll be back tomorrow, Mrs. Park. Thanks for today's lesson." She raised her hand in farewell and was halfway out the door when she doubled back. "Oh! If you want to look into the thing about the wights causing psychological trauma, check out the work of Gary and Melissa Kimball. They're on YouTube and stuff. Okay, bye!" Then she disappeared out the door.

"We should probably go, too," I said. "You've been really helpful, Helen. We appreciate your time."

Lust and I got to our feet, and Helen walked us to the front door. As she was ushering us outside, she said, "Forget about the wights. Look into the city council. I'd start with Portia Cameron. She owns Cameron Realty California. The council members are supposedly all equal, but you know what they say. Some are more equal than others." She hesitated, her lips quirking into a tentative frown. "Also? Be careful. When you start looking under rocks in this town, you're gonna find a few snakes. Good luck."

She shut the door and was gone.

eleven

. . .

"**O**kay, so what's the plan?"

We were piling into the car, or at least trying to. The cameramen were having trouble loading their equipment into the backseat. I tapped my fingers impatiently on the steering wheel as I waited for them. The network really should have gotten us a larger vehicle. "I was thinking we should go back to the restaurant. Now that we have that lead about the city council, I'd like to ask Eric and Linda about it."

"Good idea. While we're there, we should pick up that spooky soundtrack they play in the dining room. If someone embedded subliminal suggestions in it, at least we can prevent further hallucinations from happening."

The cameramen were finally locked and loaded, and I pulled out into the street. "I have no idea how to tell if an audio file's been tampered with. Any ideas?"

Lust perked up. "Oh, sure. When we get back to the house, I'll ask Wrath to analyze it for us."

I groaned, mouth twisting like I'd tasted something

bad. "Wrath? I don't know if I want his help. He called you a nympho at dinner last night."

"I am a nympho," Lust said, not missing a beat. "Plus, I'm sure I can get Wrath to do anything. Of all the housemates, I bet he's the most susceptible to my feminine wiles."

I didn't like Wrath, but I also didn't like the idea of Lust using her powers against our housemates. It felt wrong. "I don't know if that's a good idea. Envy explained your power to me, so I know it's not foolproof, but—"

"Good grief, Pride." Lust's laugh was deep and throaty. It was the type of laugh that turns heads, the type of laugh that makes other women uncomfortable, the type of laugh that gets husbands in trouble with their wives. "I don't have to use my powers on Wrath. All I have to do is this." She tugged down the front of her t-shirt, revealing an impressive amount of cleavage. "They're called boobs, honey."

My eyes lingered on her exposed bosom a second too long, and by the time I caught myself, Lust was already chuckling and tugging her top back into place. I cleared my throat and refocused on the road. "Anyway, why would we get Wrath's help? Is he a sound engineer or something?"

My partner cocked an eyebrow. "Oh, you don't know? Then I won't tell you. It'll be more fun when you discover it for yourself."

While I drove to Wights and Wongs, Lust pulled out her phone and tapped something in. After a minute, she angled her body toward me, gathering her hair over one shoulder, stroking the strands absently. "Hey, Pride, listen to this. This is what the Kimballs have to say about the wights. 'While often considered a nuisance, wights are some of the most biologically evolved non-corporeal supernatural creatures.' " Lust snickered. "Can you call a non-corporeal being biologically evolved? Is that even a thing?"

She had a point. "Bad choice of words, maybe. Keep reading."

She cleared her throat. " 'They first appeared in ancient Egypt as guardians of the pharaoh's tomb. They protected the dead from being pillaged by the living. Archaeologists believe wights contracted their services to the royal family. Today, wights are sometimes coerced or tricked into serving similar contracts. However, the nature of their services ranges from protection to simple housework. Due to these circumstances, wights have developed the ability to psychologically manipulate their human cohabitators to drive them to madness. In some cases, wights have been known to *curse their human cohabitators* to earn their freedom.' "

"Interesting," I said. "Does it explain how the curse works?"

Lust shook her head. "No, but there's more. 'While wights can and do manipulate their human cohabitators, psychological influence works the other way as well. Some people have reported that soothing music and daily affirmations can calm an agitated wight, while heavy metal music and shouting can incite anger and rebellion in these naturally non-violent creatures.' "

Lust looked up from her phone, chewing on her lips in thought. "Have you ever heard of this before?"

I shook my head. "No, but I've never researched wights before, either."

We arrived at Wights and Wongs where Linda was working at the reception desk. When she saw us, a blush crept up her cheeks. She stammered, glancing around at the empty room. "I had to send our day hostess home. There's not enough work to justify…well. Are you here to eat?"

"We were just at Helen Park's place," I said. "She said you've been having trouble with the city council."

Anger flashed behind Linda's eyes, but it quickly gave way to annoyance. "Portia Cameron is a pain in the rear," Linda grunted. "But she has bigger fish to fry than running me out of business."

"Like what?"

She ticked off the fish that needed frying on her fingers. "There's the growing homelessness problem that needs to be addressed. Our crime rate has been steadily climbing as our population increases. We don't have enough room at the high school for the number of new students we get each year. The city council seems to forget that along with growing our population and tax base—the only thing they really care about—they're also inviting more problems. Rumor is, Portia Cameron is thinking about running for mayor next year. If she wants to do that, she has to address the problems our city faces. They won't go away on their own. The last thing she needs to worry about is my little Chinese restaurant."

I was about to ask another question about the city council when the doorbell tinkled, and a delivery man walked in carrying a large box. "Excuse me a moment," she said. To the delivery guy, she asked, "Is that my order from Peteman's?"

The delivery guy nodded. "Want me to put it in the freezer for you?"

Linda shook her head. "Nah, I've got some other stuff I need to organize back there. Just set it down, and I'll deal with it in a minute. Thanks, Randy."

Randy set the box on the floor, and when he stood up, he looked Lust up and down with an expression like a dog eyeing a prime rib. He rubbed his palm on his pant leg and then extended his hand to Lust, ignoring me altogether. "Hi, there. Never seen you before. You must be new in town. I'm Randy."

Lust purred her response as she shook his hand. "Yes, you sure are."

The delivery man flushed and looked back at Linda. "Have a good day, Ms. Wong." He tucked his chin to his chest as he strode out the front door with Lust and Linda giggling in his wake.

"That wasn't nice," I said.

"But it *was* funny," Linda giggled. "And he deserved it. Randy's married with three kids. Look, Portia Cameron is a dead end," she said. "I've considered that possibility already. What else did you find out at Helen's?"

"Ruby was there," Lust said. "She seems to think the problem isn't a person in town. She thinks it's the wights themselves."

Linda sniggered, shaking her head. "My daughter spends too much time on Reddit," she said. "She needs to stop listening to charlatans trying to make names for themselves. It's not the wights," Linda repeated. "It's Helen Park."

I still wasn't convinced that Helen Park had anything to do with this, but I didn't have enough evidence to rule her out, either. I was working from my gut, and while my intuition was good, it was no substitute for hard evidence. Then I remembered my encounter with Jack Dempsey. "Another lead we're following is your audio," I said, pointing to the ceiling. A haunted organ was playing something chilling over the speakers. "It's possible someone embedded subliminal messages in the music. It's a thing con men do, and apparently, it isn't very difficult."

Linda looked up, her brows furrowed. "We've been using the same audio track for, I don't know, as long as we've been at this location. I can't imagine anybody would bother to tamper with it, but if you think it will help, I'm happy to hand it over."

I nodded. "Yeah, great. We'll look at it and see what we find."

Linda leaned over to pick up the box and jerked her head toward the back, indicating we should follow. "The audio's in the office. Come on back with me, and I'll get it for you."

We wended through the dining room, cutting through the kitchen. Wights appeared at odd intervals, their green eyes glowing in the dim light. Although I was used to seeing the human dead wandering the streets, I was unnerved to see spectral beings floating around a restaurant as servants. As I passed them, the chill of their presence sent shivers down my spine. I couldn't help but wonder if they were messing with my mind.

Would they make me see things that weren't there?

Between them and Lust, I needed to keep on my toes.

Once in the office, Linda dropped the box on her desk and then moved to the corner of the room where an ancient stereo was hooked up to what I assumed was the restaurant audio system. She ejected a disc, and my jaw dropped open. "You're still using CDs?" I said, incredulous. "I haven't seen one of these since I was a kid."

Linda chuckled as she handed me the disc. I handled it carefully, treating it like the prehistoric relic it was. "That's the only copy I have, so be careful with it. If you find anything, let me know. Hey, do me a favor? Help me with this box. My shoulders have been giving me trouble, and I need to get it in the freezer. It's fish," she said, wrinkling her nose, undoubtedly imagining the stink it would make if the fish started to defrost.

I handed the CD to Lust and hefted the box up onto my hip. I followed Linda back into the kitchen, which was occupied only by the sous chef, Ping, and an assistant cook. Linda guided me over to the large walk-in freezer and pulled on the handle to open it. She had hardly stepped inside when she let loose a bloodcurdling scream.

Adrenaline pulsed through my body, and I snapped into action, dropping the box and elbowing my way past

Linda. I stepped into the freezer and blinked, letting my eyes adjust to the dim light. I followed Linda's gaze to the floor and froze. When I was sure I was seeing what I thought I was seeing, I fished my phone out of my pocket and dialed.

"Hello?"

"Hey, Sloth? Is this you?"

"Yeah, it's me. Who's this?"

"It's Pride. Listen. Are you still looking for that guy? The old lady's missing son or whatever?"

Sloth sighed heavily into the receiver. "We're still looking, but no dice so far. We're *totally* gonna lose this challenge. I don't think Envy or Gluttony cares, either. I don't even know why they're *on* the show if they're not gonna try to win." She paused long enough to sigh again, more dramatically this time. "Why do you ask?"

I glanced over my shoulder at the shadowy area Linda was still staring at, hands pressed to her mouth in horror. "I think I found him."

Sloth gasped. "You did? Where?"

"At Wights and Wongs. The Chinese place."

On the other end, Sloth cursed under her breath. "You gotta be kidding me! Really? He just waltzed in there to have lunch? God, what rotten luck. Do you think we'll get credit even though our team didn't find him? Should I call Tricia? I should've known we'd—"

"He's not having lunch," I said. "He's in the freezer." I paused and toed the corpse with my shoe. It was frozen solid. "This probably goes without saying, but I'm pretty sure he's dead."

twelve

. . .

The sound of sirens briefly proceeded a bevy of cops pouring through the front doors. The film crew did their best to stay out of the way while also trying to get the best shots they could. Lust and I retreated to the corner of the main dining room, away from the commotion. Eric, Linda, Ping, and the assistant cook whose name I still didn't know huddled together in a booth opposite ours, swearing, crying, and barking orders. Police were taping things off, snapping photos, and strutting around like peacocks. I wondered idly when they'd last seen anything as major as an actual murder in Odyssey. They all had that "kid in a candy store" look about them.

Which was an entirely different look than the one the Wongs were sporting. Linda's face was pale, her cheeks tear-stained. Every so often, she crumpled against her husband, who cooed soothing words to her and stroked her hair, trying his best to be the rock she needed him to be. But he, too, had a haunted look in his eyes.

I guess it wasn't every day you found a corpse in your freezer.

Eventually, a lanky cop approached us, retrieving a pencil tucked behind his ear and flipping open a notebook. I didn't know cops still did that. I figured even the Odyssey PD had gone digital. He pointed the pencil at Lust and me. "You the two that found Walter?"

"Walter?"

The cop raised a brow at me. "You're not from Odyssey."

"I know that," I said, frowning.

The cop's mouth twitched in a half-grin. "The dead fella is Walter Romanowsky. Local weirdo. Thinks he's a hunter. You the two that found him?"

I shot a glance over toward the Wongs. "Linda and I found him," I said.

The cop narrowed his eyes at Lust, his gaze traveling inevitably to her bosom before he reluctantly turned his eyes to me. "What were you doing when you found the corpse?"

"Putting fish in the freezer."

The cop clucked his tongue. "Right. You notice anything strange?"

I paused. "Just the dead body in the freezer," I said.

The cop glowered at me, and I returned his stare, unblinking. I didn't know why cops asked stupid questions if they didn't want stupid answers. He cleared his throat, continuing. "We found a cat carrier in the kitchen. The staff say it's not theirs. The Wongs also don't recognize it. Does it belong to you? Did you or she —" he gestured at Lust without looking directly at her— "bring that here?"

I shook my head. "A cat carrier? No. I don't have a cat. I don't even like cats." I paused, thinking. "Did you know cats are the only mammals that can't taste sweetness? I don't trust anything that doesn't like sugar."

I must've gotten that information from the ghost girl at some point, though I don't know why I brought it up just then. Nerves, maybe. Or maybe the wights were getting to me.

My stomach roiled at the idea.

But anyway, if the cop noticed my mental deterioration, he didn't let on. "You're not going anywhere, are you? No sudden travel coming up? You'll stay in town to answer any questions, won't you?"

I donned my best pie-eating grin. "I'll be here if you need me, Officer. Happy to serve."

"Don't be a smartass," the cop said. "I'll be in touch."

Lust and I hung around long enough to ensure neither Linda nor Eric needed anything more from us before we left. When we arrived back at the house, news of the corpse in the freezer had preceded us. As soon as we stepped through the front door, the questions started.

"Was there really a freaking body at the restaurant? Holy smokes! How can anyone be so incompetent they overlooked *that?*"

"Did you see his face? Who was it?"

"Was it gross? Oh my God, I bet it was so gross. I

can't *believe* you got to see a frozen corpse and I didn't. Some people have all the luck!"

Lust and I took turns fielding questions as Gluttony hustled to and from the kitchen, bringing snacks and beverages to everyone. For himself, he'd brought out an entire gallon of ice cream, which he proceeded to eat with a giant spoon as he plopped down beside Wrath on the couch. "How did you know the dead guy was our missing person?"

"Sloth showed me his photo. He was wearing the same camouflage hunting suit. So unless there's a lot of guys in town running around like that, I was pretty sure it was him."

"I expect the police will tell the public before long." Envy was studying her phone, scrolling endlessly. "Social media's already hashtagging the department asking who it was. God, poor Mrs. Romanowsky." She curled forward, sinking her chin into her hand. "She's been trying to get the police to look for her son since before we got here. And now he shows up dead? I hope she sues them into oblivion."

Silence settled over the room, punctuated only by the sounds of chewing and slurping. Gluttony had graced us with another amazing meal, though I wasn't sure what magic he'd put in this one. Sometimes good food is just good food.

"Do you think our two cases are related?" Sloth peeled off her socks as she asked this, dropping them to the floor. "Like, if you're trying to put a restaurant out of business, no better way than to stuff a dead body in the freezer. I can't imagine people will want to eat somewhere a murder occurred." She threw a sideways glance at Wrath. "Stop thinking about me," she hissed.

"I can't help it!" Wrath gestured wildly to the dirty socks on the floor. "You just drop your nasty, sweaty, *disgusting* socks in the middle of our living room, and you act like it's no big deal! It's gross, Sloth! Everybody else is thinking it, too; they're just too polite to say anything!"

"They *weren't* thinking it before," Sloth said, her own anger rising. "But they are thinking it now!"

"Nobody would be thinking anything if you weren't such a pig!"

Lust tapped me on the knee, and I peeled my eyes away from the growing pile of laundry Sloth was accumulating on the floor. She'd just unclasped her bra, pulled it out through an armhole, and dropped it on top of her socks. "Do you think the wights had anything to do with this?"

I snickered. "Wights? Come on. No."

Lust looked surprised. "Why are you so sure? You don't think wights can drag a person into a freezer?"

I thought about the ghost girl I'd tried to entertain over the years. For the most part, she was incapable of interacting with the physical world. "Seems unlikely. They don't have bodies. How would they drag a fully grown man into a freezer?"

"They serve food, though," Lust pointed out. "So they can carry things. Who's to say how strong they are?"

I frowned. I hadn't thought about that. "Still. I don't think—"

"And maybe they didn't drag him in there at all.

Maybe they lured him in there. Or," Lust said, her face going serious, "maybe they used mental manipulation to get him in there. Either way, once he was inside, all they'd have to do is close the door."

I dismissed these ideas with a wave of my hand. "If that was the case, the victim could just *open* the door. Industrial freezers can be opened from inside," I reminded her.

Lust hesitated, then whispered, "Mental manipulation, Pride. Hypnosis. Plain old fear."

I was uncomfortable with these speculations, but Lust was right—I had no reason to think the wights couldn't have murdered this person. My skepticism had little to do with facts and more to do with my feelings. I didn't want to believe anyone could be manipulated into walking into a death trap. The idea that wights could do that was terrifying to me.

But it was more than that. The idea that *Lust* might be able to do that was terrifying to me.

Sloth chewed on the end of her pigtail as she dug her bare feet into the crevice between the couch cushions. "What mental manipulation?"

Lust explained what she'd read about manipulation and curses on the Kimball's website. When she finished, she shrugged. "It seems plausible is all I'm saying."

Sloth frowned. "Could just be propaganda. Or, you know. Total BS."

I laughed, wagging a finger in Lust's face. "Never get too excited about a theory," I said. "Your pet theories will almost always turn out to be BS."

Lust ignored me and turned to Wrath. "Hey. I need a favor."

Wrath's scowl immediately slid into a grin, eyebrows arching on his face. "Oh yeah? What's up?"

Lust smiled playfully, her finger trailing lightly over her lips. "You're pretty handy with technology stuff, right? If I gave you a CD, do you think you could analyze it and see if anybody tampered with it?"

"Tampered with it how?"

Lust shrugged seductively. "Like, could you find an embedded message if it was there?"

Wrath nodded, his eyes glued to Lust's chest. "Yeah, sure, man. I can do that. Easy. I thought you had a challenge for me."

Boobs, I thought as Lust dropped me an I-told-you-so wink. *They really do work.* I shook off my dismay. "So, is that your day job? Are you a sound engineer or something?"

Instead of answering, Wrath pointed to the television. The power was off. "Channel 4," he said. At his command, the television flickered to life. An anchorwoman was standing before a camera at Wights and Wongs, reporting on what we had just seen with our own eyes. The ticker across the bottom read, "Man found dead in Chinese restaurant freezer."

"How did you—"

Wrath pointed to the smartwatch I wore at my wrist. "Text a message from Pride's girlfriend," he said.

Now, my smartwatch buzzed and lit up with a new message. Stunned, I looked down to see a message from

Shayda lighting up the watch face. It read, "I'm not coming back. Get your life together, Sid."

I dropped my hand into my lap, my mouth agape as I stared at Wrath. "How did you do that? What the hell was that?"

Wrath looked very pleased with himself as he linked his hands behind his head and leaned back into the cushions. "I'm a technopath, man. I can get technology to do anything I want."

"This is quite serious, you know." Greed ambled into the room, hands tucked casually into his pockets. "The situation with the Wongs. You should let the police handle it. They're trained for this kind of thing. You're not. You'll just get in the way."

"I know how to stay out of the way during an ongoing investigation," I said. "I assist the police on cases like this all the time."

"Excellent!" Greed clapped his palms and rubbed them together. "Then you don't need us. You should already have the resources you require, right?"

"I don't need *you*," I agreed warily. "I need *Wrath*. What do you care anyway? Why—"

I stopped short as understanding dawned. Greed was Wrath's partner. They hadn't completed their task yet, whatever it was, and Greed didn't want Wrath's attention divided. Greed wanted to win—or at least, to beat us.

Lust figured it out the same time I did. "You're a schmuck," she said, lip curling.

"Might be, but I'm a schmuck that isn't gonna let you horn in on my victory. Nobody on our task is dead, so it stands to reason we should win this round. As long as Bottle Blond over there doesn't blow his cool or waste time solving other people's cases, we've got this in the bag."

Envy wriggled to the edge of the sofa, showing her palms as she gaped. "Do you know how heartless you look right now? A person is frozen as solid as a grocery store turkey, and you're talking about winning a stupid competition?"

"Hey, if it's so stupid, feel free to drop out any time," Greed crooned, that slimy smile growing wider. "You all knew what you were getting into when you signed the contract. The rest of you might be in this to play Good Samaritan, but I'm in it to win. I intend to be America's favorite sin, and I won't let any of you jackholes get in my way."

And with that, Greed backed away, flashed double peace signs, and left.

With Greed gone, Lust returned her attention to Wrath. "So, about the audio—"

"Yeah, yeah," he cut in with a sigh. "I'll get to it when I can."

Lust batted her lashes. "Thank you."

Wrath scowled. "Don't mention it. Especially to Greed."

"I hate that guy," Sloth said to no one in particular. Then, turning to me, she asked, "So what's your plan? Are you guys gonna keep trying to solve the fortune cookie thing or what?"

"The way I see it, the Wongs are in an even worse position than before," I said. "If people weren't saying the place was cursed before, they'll start now. So, I'd like to keep working on it." I turned to Lust. "I mean, if you do. I'll understand if you don't want to touch this with a ten-foot pole."

But Lust waved that away. "Like hell am I dropping out now. I'm with you, Pride. Whether these cases are connected or not, *something* bizarre is going on here. I want to find out what it is."

That was a relief. I *could* continue investigating on my own, but having Lust around would likely make it easier. She had skills I could use, as much as I hated to admit it.

Plus, I enjoyed her company, which I hated to admit even worse.

"All right, then. I guess you know what we need to do first." When Lust just stared at me blankly, I said, "We have to interview Walter."

Lust continued staring. A long moment passed before she stated, "He's dead, Pride."

I grinned. Not because it was a funny situation—it wasn't, and I knew that. I'm awkward, not a moron— but because she looked so concerned, like maybe she was wondering if I actually *was* a moron. "That's okay. I'm a ghost whisperer. If the dead have secrets, I'm the one to find them."

thirteen

. . .

I'd been to the city morgue plenty of times, but never without the police department's blessing. I was relatively sure I didn't stand a snowball's chance in hell of getting to the corpses on my own, so I took some precautions and dressed for the occasion. I traded in my old jeans and t-shirt for proper slacks, a sensible shirt with actual buttons, and ditched my Chucks for the only nice shoes I owned. I felt like a tool, but when Lust saw me, she whistled, her eyebrows leaping toward her hairline. "Well, hello, Pride! You clean up good! Why do you look so spiffy?"

"I don't know if this will actually work," I said, tucking my shirt into my pants. "But you know how people are. Easily tricked by appearances. I figure this whole thing might go smoother if I look professional."

"Not a bad idea," she said. "What about me? How do I look?"

You know that expression "like a deer in headlights"? I imagine that's how I looked at that moment as

I searched for the right response to this question. The truth was a no-go: Lust looked like she was auditioning to be the first person killed in a horror movie. Her shorts were so short, the pocket lining peeked out from beneath the hem. Her blouse—if you could call it that—exposed most of her midriff and an amount of cleavage that would have made the devil blush.

On the other hand, she had a part to play, and if she did need to seduce someone, well, at least she'd have an advantage.

"Charming," I said finally. Which was true, depending on your definition of "charm." "Let's go."

On the other side of the room, one of the film crew started moving toward me, but I held up my hand, palm out. "Not this time," I said.

The cameraman clucked his teeth. "You know the deal. Where you go, I go."

"Today, where I go could get you arrested," I said. I noticed how Lust stiffened at that. "You're way too conspicuous with that camera. You're not coming with me, and that's final. Take it up with Tricia later if you want."

"Do us both a favor, then," he said. He gestured toward my pocket. "Video it for me. On your phone. The network might be able to use that footage at least."

I felt my pocket to make sure I had my phone, gave a crisp salute in agreement, and then we were off.

Seaside County didn't have its own morgue, so homicide victims were taken to the morgue at the local hospital. I didn't know precisely where the Odyssey morgue was, but most hospital morgues were in the basement, so that's where we headed. Inside the elevator, I dug out my phone. I scanned the Odyssey General website, hoping to find the morgue attendant's name. I flipped through three pages before I found it. Dennis Parker. Bingo.

As the elevator made its slow descent, I prepped Lust for how this would all go down. "What we're hoping for today is run-of-the-mill incompetence," I explained. "Homicide victims are supposed to go straight into the tank, where they're locked up until it's time to autopsy them. That way, unscrupulous people like you or me can't waltz in and start messing with them. To get into the crypt, you need the right credentials, which we don't have. So, the first thing we'll try is the 'act like you own the place' method."

"Okay." She swallowed hard before asking, "What's that?"

"It's where you just walk in and act like you own the place," I said. Really, that seemed self-evident. "People are tricked by confidence. It works in some cases, but I doubt it's gonna work for us here. Still, it's worth a try."

Lust blew out a puff of hot air and fidgeted with her hair. By now, I was getting familiar with her tells: she was nervous. Nervous was no good. Nervous people didn't look like they owned the place. I clasped her by the shoulder and gave a little squeeze. "You can do this," I said. "But you have to act natural."

Lust bobbed her head up and down, but it wasn't exactly in agreement. "And if it doesn't work? What's Plan B?"

I wasn't so sure I really had a Plan A, so calling our

failure option Plan B was maybe giving ourselves too much credit, but I let it slide. "Then we wing it. If you can charm the attendant into letting us in, you do that. If not?" I shrugged. "We'll cross that bridge when we come to it." When the elevator doors opened and we stepped out, I added. "Also, when we get to the stiffs, please try not to throw up."

I followed the signs that directed us to the morgue. I pushed through the heavy double doors that separated the respectable part of the hospital wing from the place nobody wanted to visit. I walked past a reception desk on my right, repeating silently to myself, *I own the place. I own the place. I own—*

"Ah, excuse me? You there?" The woman behind the desk was on her feet, waving a hand at me, her expression pinched. "Where do you think you're going? You can't go in there."

I looked around, pretending to be confused as I donned my best award-winning grin. "Eh? What's the problem? I was just going to see Dennis." I jammed my thumb over my shoulder in the general direction I hoped Dennis was. For that matter, I hoped Dennis still worked here. Hospital websites were notoriously unreliable.

The attendant shook her head, all business. "Authorized personnel only, no exceptions." She looked me up and down before doing the same to Lust. Neither outfit seemed to impress her, and I felt our chances of slipping into the crypt evaporating by the second. "Look, I don't know what you're playing at. But you're not getting in there. Don't make me call security."

Calling security would be bad, so I eased up on the fake charm and headed back in the same direction we'd come from. "No problem. I'll just give Dennis a ring. I'm okay to stay out in the hallway, aren't I?"

The woman shrugged. "Suit yourself."

I took a quick inventory of her desk before Lust and I pushed back through the double doors, regrouping in the hallway.

Lust leaned against a wall as a fluorescent light flickered overhead. "Okay, so now what do we do? I can try to charm her, but I don't think it'll work. She didn't seem to like my outfit."

I rejected the suggestion with a flick of my fingers. "Too risky. If it doesn't work, she'll definitely call security, and then we're toast. But I think we might be in luck. I noticed a keycard on her desk. She wasn't wearing it around her neck like she's supposed to. Remember what I said when we got here? We're hoping for basic, run-of-the-mill incompetence."

Lust chewed her lip and peered over my shoulder, looking through the windows on the double doors we had just passed through. "I don't know, Pride. She seemed pretty serious about doing her job."

I, too, turned to look over my shoulder, peering through the glass. From my vantage point, I could just barely see the woman sitting behind her desk, rifling through papers. I cracked my knuckles and heaved a sigh. "You don't have anywhere else to be, do you?"

Lust frowned. "No, why?"

"Because I have a feeling we might be here a while. We're just gonna have to wait."

Lust held her hands out, imploring. "Wait for what?"

"For nature to call. We're gonna stake out the place until she has to go to the bathroom."

Lust exhaled, running a hand through her hair. "Well, poop."

"Yes," I agreed. "Hopefully sooner than later."

I had to admit, staking out a hospital morgue was incredibly boring. There were no people to watch, and Lust and I ran out of conversation pretty quickly. Even social media wasn't holding my interest. After 45 minutes, I started to seriously question whether the morgue attendant was getting enough water in her diet when, blessedly, she finally got up from her seat. My heart skipped a beat when I saw her reach for the keycard on her desk. If she took the keycard with her, we had just wasted a bunch of time. But she reached past it and grabbed her purse, tucking it under her arm and heading for what I presumed was the ladies' room.

When the attendant was out of sight, I grabbed Lust by the wrist, and we pushed through the doors. I lifted the keycard from the desk and hurried through the halls, looking for the crypt.

We'd turned down several hallways and tried several locked doors when I found it. "This is it," I said, stopping at an unmarked door decorated only with a keycard reader. Lust sidled up behind me so close, I could feel her breath at my back. She squeezed my elbow, her nails digging into my skin.

I swiped the card, breath held. To be honest, I wasn't 100% sure this was the right door. For all I knew, I could have just swiped into the admin break room. We could be about to walk in on a clandestine game of strip poker. You wouldn't believe some of the stories I've heard about what goes on behind the scenes in the morgue.

The door beeped.

I turned the handle and pushed open the door. We stepped into a refrigerated room, and I shivered both with cold and relief. No strip poker. Just dead bodies.

Lots of them.

We were surrounded by corpses. Some were wrapped in heavy plastic and tied up with rope. Those were the bodies that had already been autopsied and were awaiting transport somewhere else. But many of the bodies were merely draped in a shroud. That's what we were looking for. Unless, of course, the city's administrators had actually done their jobs and took our victim to the tank. I crossed my fingers and hoped again for run-of-the-mill incompetence.

I looked over at Lust, whose skin had blanched to near colorlessness. "You okay?" I asked.

She swallowed and swayed on her feet. "I will be. Let's just get on with this and get out of here as soon as we can."

I paused, remembering what the camera guy had requested. "Maybe you should film this," I said. "If we don't bring back any footage, the network goons might insist on tagging along next time. Assuming there's a next time."

Lust looked a little green around the gills, but she dug out her phone anyway and held it up, framing the shot. She brushed the hair from her eyes and said, "Ready when you are."

We moved quickly from body to body, flipping tags and reading names. How did a town as small as Odyssey have so many bodies waiting to be autopsied? I thought of Helen Park and her admonishment to be careful lest we overturn the wrong rock and uncover some nasty snakes. A shiver ran down my spine. I was beginning to think there was more to Odyssey, California, than they advertised on the billboards plastered along Pacific Coast Highway.

As I was contemplating all this, Lust's voice cut through the silence. "Found him."

I strode over to where she was standing. Sure enough, the tag around his toe read, "Walter Romanowsky." Gingerly, I moved Lust aside as I drew nearer the corpse. As I reached out to remove the shroud, Lust grabbed my hand. "Wait." She licked her lips, unsure. "Aren't you worried about fingerprints or something?"

I hesitated, curling my fingers into my palm. I hadn't worried about that in the past because I'd been working with the police. But this time, I could be putting myself in jeopardy. And the last thing I needed was legal trouble on top of everything else.

Still, I had a job to do. And not just for the Wongs, either. The wrongful dead had stories to tell. They deserved to be heard.

I flexed my fingers and blew out a sigh. "It can't be helped, Lust. I have to touch him for my ability to kick in. Let's just hope for the best." I closed my eyes and brought my hands to the corpse's cheeks, pressing my palms against the cold, gray skin.

Slowly, the Wong's kitchen glimmered into view. I was inside Walt's memory, seeing things from his perspective. He sauntered into the kitchen to find Ping coming out of the Wongs' office, something clutched in her hand. When she saw Walt, she drew up short, her free hand pressed against her heart. Her muscles were stiff, her face drawn into an expression I couldn't read. Her lips moved—she was talking, but I couldn't hear the conversation. The longer the discussion wore on, the more Ping fidgeted, shifting her weight from foot to foot. She chewed on her lips, eyes darting around the room.

And then, without warning, Ping stepped over to the stove and lifted a frying pan. Walter closed the distance between them in a few long strides. Ping swiveled, bringing the pan down on Walter's head.

Everything went black.

I pulled my hands away from the cadaver and folded them against my chest. Lust stepped closer, closing her fingers around my upper arm. "Pride? Did it work? What did you see?"

I groaned, scrubbing over my eyes before I remembered I'd just been touching a corpse, and dropped my hands quickly to my sides. "Damn, Lust. Maybe it's not our lucky day after all."

fourteen

. . .

"Ping? No, that's impossible. There has to be some kind of mistake."

A few days had passed since we'd sneaked into the hospital morgue, and Lust and I were sitting across from Mr. and Mrs. Wong at the restaurant. We had Sloth along with us, too, because it was mostly her case. Plus, I suspected that her ability to peek inside other people's minds might come in handy.

I folded my hands on the table and leaned forward, giving my head a slow but certain shake. "I'm sorry, Linda. But I saw with my own two eyes. My own two mind's eyes?" I glanced at Lust to see if the joke landed, but she just stared at me with a "What are you doing?" look on her face, so I guess it didn't. "Anyway, the point is, I'm not wrong about these things. I touched Walt's face, and I saw Ping. Clear as day. She hit him over the head with a cast-iron frying pan."

I knew this was a lot of information for the Wongs to take in. I couldn't blame them for not wanting to face the facts, especially if Ping was the superstar asset they believed she was. Linda was looking at her husband, eyes wide and unblinking. Her mouth was working, but words weren't coming out.

"It's just that we've known Ping for years, and she doesn't have it in her," Eric said. "She doesn't have a violent bone in her body! Besides, what would be her motive?"

"Well, that's what I'm here to find out," I said. "I'd like to talk to her if you don't mind. I know I should probably leave this to the police, but between you and me, I'm not so sure the officials in this town are all that capable."

Snickers of agreement went around the table. "You don't have to convince us that the people running this city leave much to be desired," Eric chortled under his breath. "Still, I agree with my wife. There has to be some mistake about Ping. I trust her utterly. She can't have done this. She just can't."

"We just want to talk to her," Lust said, her voice melodious and even. "And we promise, we won't say anything to the police if you don't want us to. We're doing this for *you*. You deserve answers, and we want to find them."

Linda Wong squared her shoulders and tossed her hair away from her face. "Okay. Fine. If nothing else, maybe talking to Ping will prove that you must've misunderstood what you saw. You'll see. She's not the person you say she is."

We found Ping in the kitchen stir-frying something at the stove, expression grim and focused as she worked the wok. She wore a neat, floral print dress with a long, white apron. Her hair, an eye-catching auburn shot through with silver, was tucked into a hairnet. When she saw us, she turned off the stove and stepped away, frowning. She glanced from Eric to Linda and back again. "Is something the matter?"

Linda gestured in my direction. "Ping, these people would like to have a word with you. They have some questions about what happened the other night." She swallowed and tried on a smile, but it didn't stick, sliding off her lips almost as quickly as it had appeared. "Why don't you all step into my office? I'll handle the kitchen the best I can."

At first, Ping didn't move except to brush her hands along her apron, fidgeting. Finally, she nodded, lips twitching. "Sure. Okay." She patted her hairnet, checking that everything was still in place.

Lust, Sloth, and I followed Ping into a small office at the back of the kitchen. My housemates took their seats, but Ping and I remained standing. I closed the door behind us, giving us a bit of privacy. "Ping," I said. "I have some questions about the murder."

Ping's troubled expression deepened. "Murder?" Her voice was high and squeaky. "The police said it might have been an accident."

I linked my hands in front of me and dropped my gaze. "I haven't spoken to the police," I admitted. "That's not why I'm here. I'm a psychic. When I touch people, I see things. When I touch dead people, I often see the last thing they saw before they died." I paused, hoping to see a flicker of something in Ping's eyes—guilt or confusion, maybe. But she remained stoic, so I pressed on. "I went to see Walt in the morgue. I laid my hands on his face. And what I saw…"

I had everyone's rapt attention. Lust and Sloth were both staring at me, eyes wide, perched on the edge of their seats. Before now, I had only given Lust the barest details. Now, I was about to detail exactly what I'd seen. Ping had to know. More importantly, I wanted to see how she reacted. And I wanted Sloth to have good context for when she rooted around in Ping's gray matter.

"I saw you, Ping. I saw you clear as day. I could tell that you were talking, but I can't hear in my visions. I only see. So I don't know what you or Walt said, but I know you were the last person he saw before he died. You hit him in the head with a frying pan. I saw the whole thing. Walt never woke up after that."

Everyone was still. I heard nothing but the whirring of the air conditioner and the pounding of my heart against my eardrums. And then, as if breaking free of a spell, Ping erupted into tears.

"I don't know what you're talking about!" she wailed. "I don't know why you're doing this. I don't know what you're trying to prove here. I had nothing to do with Walter's death. Nothing! It wasn't me!"

Lust dug into her purse and pulled out a tissue, which she handed to Ping. The older woman accepted gratefully, blowing her nose while she trembled. "I don't have any reason to hurt Walter," she said. "There has to be another explanation. I don't know anything about psychics or visions, but *surely* you make mistakes. I could never kill anyone."

I nodded slowly. "Well, you're right about one thing. There is another explanation. After you hit Walt in the head with a frying pan—that part's not up for debate, Ping, I *saw* it—he could have just fallen unconscious. Someone else could have dragged him into the freezer."

This concession seemed to reinvigorate Ping, who was nodding frantically. "Okay, yes! It had to be someone else, right? Someone else who stuffed the body into the freezer?"

"It *could* be," I stipulated, "but besides you and the Wongs, who else has after-hours access to the restaurant?"

"The wights do," Lust said, her voice soft.

I swiveled, throwing her my best "What are *you* doing?" look, but she ignored me. She was gazing at Ping. "Ping, have you ever noticed the wights acting strangely? Agitated or violent? Anything like that?"

Ping's mouth worked, lips twitching as the cords in her neck strained. She swallowed several times before shaking her head, her shoulders slumped. "No. I wish I could say yes. That would be much better for me." Her voice broke as she choked down a fresh sob. "But I don't like to lie. I've never seen the wights do anything but serve food."

Silence grew thick between us, and after a while, Lust stood from her chair and walked over to the crying woman, enveloping her in a hug. She stroked her back and squeezed her arm until Ping's crying subsided. I had to give her credit. Lust was a lot better at dealing with people than I was. Which I guess wasn't saying much.

"Let's start at the beginning," Lust said. "Did you know Walter?"

Ping bobbed her head side to side, dithering. "Not personally. I knew *of* him. Everyone does. He's a bit of a legend in this town."

That piqued my curiosity. "A legend? How so?"

Now, Ping rolled her eyes and sniffled, swiping at a drop of liquid falling from a nostril. "Well, you've seen him. He wore that weird camo outfit pretty much all the time. He lived with his mom. He claimed to be a hunter, but there's nowhere to hunt in Odyssey, and he wasn't the outdoorsy kind, anyway. You know what I mean? He was pretty much a loner. A very eccentric, creepy loner." She gave a dry laugh, but there was no mirth in it. "Everyone in town knows he's crazy, but they give him a wide berth because his mother has money. And anyway, he's harmless. Or, was," she amended.

"Do you remember seeing him the night of the murder?"

Ping hesitated before taking the last empty seat in the executive chair behind the desk. "I...yes. I do remember seeing him," Ping admitted. "I'd come back to the restaurant late in the night after we closed. I'd left my keys behind, and I needed to come collect them. When I came in, I didn't lock the front door, so I guess he just walked in. He found me back here and started asking me weird questions."

"Lust narrowed her eyes. "What kind of weird questions?"

Ping shrugged miserably, sinking down in the chair. "I don't know. Nonsense stuff. Asking me how old I really was, where I was from, stuff like that. *Creepy* stuff like that."

Lust nodded. "That *is* creepy. No one should ask a lady how old she is. And then what happened?"

Ping hesitated, her lips parting as her eyes drifted upward as she thought. Then she shrugged, wringing her hands in her lap. "That's all I remember," she said.

"That's it?" Sloth had been quiet this whole time, but now she leaned forward, eyes glowing as she caught Ping's gaze. "You're *sure* you don't remember anything else? Maybe he attacked you? Something like that?"

But Ping was adamant, shaking her head vehemently. "No, nothing like that. He asked me a bunch of weird questions, I told him to leave me alone, and then I left. That was the end of it."

Frustrated, I blew out my cheeks. "This is a waste of time," I said, folding my arms across my chest. "I *saw* you hit Walt with a frying pan. I *saw* it."

"I don't know what you saw," the woman said, her words still thick from crying. "But I didn't hit anyone. It wasn't me."

"Okay, Ping," Lust said. "Thanks for being so cooperative. I don't know what's going to happen next," she admitted. "The police will probably want to talk to you if they haven't already. You shouldn't—"

Now, the sous chef grew frantic, a wildness growing behind her eyes that made my throat tighten. She bared her teeth in a snarl, and for a split second, she reminded me of a trapped animal. But then her fierceness melted away, and she was herself again, a small, scared slip of a woman caught in an impossible circumstance. "God, you're not going to tell them what you *think* you saw, are you? You can't do that. You might as well kill me yourself if you do that."

"Why?" It was Sloth who asked, her head titled to one side, her face open. "No, really. Why would you say that?"

"You don't know what this town's really like," Ping replied, a sharp undercurrent cutting through her words. "It's full of vipers. If you tell the police you imagined me killing Walter—"

"I didn't imagine it," I interjected.

"—they'll arrest me for sure. It'll be a witch hunt, even without evidence. I'm *Chinese*," she said. "An *immigrant*. They'd love to blame this on me. You think they'll hesitate to throw me in jail? And even if I can prove my innocence, my reputation will be destroyed. Whatever you think I did, at least don't tell the *cops*. Please."

I sighed. "Don't worry. We're not gonna tell the cops anything. But if I were you, I'd stick around and keep a low profile. Don't do anything to arouse their suspicion, like skipping town. You got it?"

Ping nodded miserably. "I got it."

I dug my hands in my pockets. "Okay. Well, best of luck to you." I jerked my head toward the door, and both housemates followed me out of the office. I spoke briefly with the Wongs in the kitchen, collecting a few more bits of information and sharing what we'd learned, which wasn't much. They thanked us, shoved the stir-fry Ping had been making into our hands, and walked us to the parking lot. We piled into the car, and only when the doors were closed did I say, "So, Sloth. What do we think of that?"

In the backseat, Sloth chewed thoughtfully on the end of her pigtail. Finally, she said, "She was telling the truth."

I turned quickly in my seat, craning my neck to get a better view of Sloth's face. "I'm sorry, *what?*"

Sloth shrugged, her face pink and splotchy. "I don't know what to tell you. I was reading her mind the whole time she was talking, and she wasn't lying. Or at least, she believed everything she was saying." She paused. "There *was* something strange, though."

I rolled my hand in a "Get on with it" motion. "Strange how? What was it?"

"When she talked about Walt asking her the creepy questions, her mind got dark and hazy. It reminded me of TV static. Or like I was watching a videotape, and someone had erased part of the film."

That *was* interesting. "Have you ever seen anything like that before?"

Sloth shook her head. "No. And that wasn't the only weird thing. Most people's thoughts are jumbled and nonlinear. People think of lots of different things at a time. They'll be talking about how much they hate their jobs, for example, but they're also thinking about what they need from the grocery store, the rent that's due, the time they lied to their spouse about why they'd come home so late, and what to get Mom for her birthday. It's all in there, jumbled together like the clearance section at Walmart."

"Okay. And her mind wasn't like that?"

"No. Ping's thoughts were very organized. *Too* organized. Like she was trying very hard to only focus on the present."

"And what do you make of that?"

Sloth shook her head again. "I don't know. I'm not a psychic detective. I can only tell you what I saw."

I turned around and started up the car, lost in my own thoughts. Ping *couldn't* be telling the truth. I'd seen her strike the victim with my own eyes. There had to be another explanation.

But then I remembered Sloth's caveat: that Ping *believed* she was telling the truth. And according to Sloth, some of her memories were missing. That might explain the contradicting facts.

I still didn't know what to make of the weirdly organized thoughts, though.

All of this wanted further investigation, but I was tired. It was all starting to feel overwhelming, the evidence spinning out of control. And though there was no hidden camera footage to corroborate my hunch— yes, I asked, I'm not *that* bad at my job—I didn't believe the wights were involved. No one else had dragged the victim into the freezer.

Ping had done that.

The question that would keep me awake that night and every night until I solved this case was—why?

fifteen

· · ·

The following day, I was surprised to find Sloth already awake and dressed when I came downstairs for breakfast. She was usually the last one up, coming to the dining room in her ratty slippers and housecoat crusted with various spilled foods. But today, she was wearing a clean sundress, sandals, and even her hair was properly brushed.

"Good morning," she chirped, handing me a mug of coffee. "How did you sleep?"

"Fine," I said, taking a careful sip. "You?"

Sloth tutted. "I've always been a poor sleeper. Being in this house doesn't make it easier. I hear people's thoughts more clearly at night. Drifting through the walls. It's disconcerting. I've asked my doc for something to help me sleep or at least block out all the constant inputs. But so far, nothing seems to work."

I gestured toward her outfit. "Is that why you're up so early? Do you have an appointment to see your doctor?"

Sloth laughed and shook her head, going to the fridge for orange juice, which she immediately sloshed onto the floor. It didn't faze her at all. She merely swatted at it with the toe of one sandal. "No, nothing like that. I was actually going over to see Walter's mom, Eleanor Romanowsky."

I retrieved a paper towel from the counter and bent down to wipe up Sloth's mess. Wrath would lose his mind if he came down later to a sticky kitchen. "Really? But your case is already solved. We found her son. Just not alive."

Sloth nodded and gulped her juice. "I know. But I guess I feel bad. When I first got assigned to her case, I made assumptions about her. I called her crazy and stuff." Sloth frowned at the memory. "I don't think she's crazy now. She suspected something was wrong, and she was right, but not a single person believed her. So, anyway, I thought it might be nice if she had some company. Someone to distract her."

I wasn't so sure that a grieving mother wanted to be distracted. Still, I couldn't deny it was a kind sentiment. "Would you mind if I tagged along? I'd like to get more information on Walt. Something personal."

Now, Sloth gave me a dubious look over the rim of her juice glass. "I don't know, Pride. You're not gonna ask her a bunch of insensitive questions and start her crying and everything, are you? I don't mean to be rude, but you're not super great with people, you know?"

She was right about that, but I was pretty sure I could be on my best behavior. "I just want to ask her some questions about her son. Find out what he was like. What were his hobbies? What was he like as a kid? Things like that. I'm not gonna ask anything pointed like what he was doing on the night of the murder."

She still looked doubtful. "You promise?"

I drew a cross over my heart and held up two fingers. "Scout's honor," I said. Which meant exactly nothing at all since I wasn't and had never been a Scout, but Sloth didn't need to know that.

My promise seemed to do the trick. Sloth's face brightened, and she nodded, slurping down the last of the juice. It dribbled down her chin, but, miraculously, she wiped it away before it ended up on her chest. "Okay then! I was going to leave now. Are you ready?"

Today was the film crew's day off. They didn't film every second of every day, and I was looking forward to a day without them. Still, I wanted to get *some* footage of the day's adventure. Just to be safe. "Let me get my phone."

A few minutes later, we were out the door and in the car, making the short drive over to Eleanor Romanowsky's house. Like Sinful House, the Romanowsky place was a few blocks from the ocean. As we emerged from our vehicle, I saw a flock of seagulls circling overhead. Not far away, ocean waves crashed on the shore. The sound of the surf was comforting. It was hard to believe we were here investigating a murder. Everything looked so peaceful.

On the other side of the street, something caught my eye. A couple was walking up the sidewalk, hand in hand, oblivious to everything except each other. I paused, watching them, a familiar shiver running down my spine. The woman looked up and saw me. When she saw that I saw her, too, she stopped in her tracks, tugging her partner back. She pointed at me. I swallowed.

"Wait a minute, Sloth," I said.

She stopped in the middle of the street, turning with her hand pressed to her forehead, making a visor above her eyes. "What is it?"

"Over there," I said, gesturing with my chin. I don't know why I did that, because Sloth couldn't see what I saw.

She looked around. "Over where?"

The couple was walking toward me now, their smiles growing wider even as my stomach rolled. I glanced from the woman to Sloth and back again. "Ghosts," I said.

Now, Sloth hurried to my side, catching me around the arm. "What? Where? What are you talking about?"

"I see them sometimes," I explained. "There's two coming toward us now. I almost missed them. They almost look alive except…"

Sloth waited, her mouth agape. When I didn't continue, she squeezed my arm tighter. "Except *what*?"

I swallowed again. "They're wearing swimsuits, and they're dripping wet. But it's their skin. Their lips. Too blue."

The color drained from Sloth's face. "Did Envy's undine get them?"

I almost laughed at the absurdity, but Sloth was very serious, and I didn't want to hurt her feelings. "No. They died by drowning."

The couple approached, and I stood still, unsure what they might want from me. Usually, ghosts ignored me completely. Other times, they were frightened and demanded help. That happened most often with the newly dead. But these two appeared neither newly dead nor distressed. Their pace was steady, and they were smiling. But the closer they came, the stranger they looked. The woman's hair was knotted with snarls of seaweed. The man's bare torso was severely abraded.

The man raised a hand in greeting. I raised mine back. "Hello there," he called. "Can you see us?"

I nodded. "I see you," I said. Even though I'd been engaging with ghosts my whole life, starting conversations with them was always awkward. You couldn't exactly ask, "How's it going?" or anything like that. It's obviously not going well, because they're dead.

"I wonder if you could help us, then," the woman said. "We…well, we're obviously dead, right?"

I nodded again. "You are. My condolences," I added.

"Oh, it's fine. We figured it out a while ago." The man put his arm around the woman and squeezed her close. "But we haven't managed to go…well, this is gonna sound stupid, but…aren't we supposed to go somewhere? Heaven or the other side or something? I mean, as nice as Odyssey is, this can't be everything, right?"

"Probably not," I agreed.

"Well, then, since you can see us, maybe you can help? Do you have…I don't know, directions? On how to find the others? The other dead, I mean?"

I sighed. I knew what they were asking. I'd been asked this at least a thousand times before. Maybe not a thousand, but many times, anyway. And even after all this time, it was a question I couldn't answer. I wasn't sure anyone could. "No, I don't. I have no idea how to get…*there.*"

Sloth squeezed my arm again. "Get where? What are they saying?"

I shushed her, keeping focused on the ghosts. Their smiles faded, and their cheeks sagged, eyes drooping at the corners. Even I recognize that disappointment, and it stabbed me right in the heart. "Okay. Well, thanks anyway. Hey, have a good rest of your day. And take it from me—steer clear of the riptides."

The ghosts retreated, turning their backs to me and continuing their walk up the street. They left the barest trace of watery footprints in their wake. A moment later, they were gone.

I turned to Sloth. "They're stranded here," I explained. "They were asking for directions to the other side. Or the afterlife. Or wherever."

Sloth's mouth dropped into an *o* as she craned her neck to look around as though maybe with this new info, she'd be able to see them. Of course, it didn't work. "Those poor things," she said, peeling herself away from me. "Why does it happen? Why do some people get stuck here after they die?"

I snorted, shaking my head. "If you find out, write a book about it. You'll be rich. It's one of the greatest paranormal questions of our lifetime."

She blinked. "Really? No one knows?"

"No one. But hey, don't let it get to you." I saw the way her lips trembled, how she reached for that pigtail to chew on. "Those two, at least, didn't seem too upset about it. They have each other."

For a moment, Sloth looked doubtful. But then she shrugged it off and nodded, confirming something to herself. "You're right. We have other things to worry about. Let's see Mrs. Romanowsky."

———

Sloth rang the doorbell. A few moments later, the door creaked open, and a small, gray-haired woman appeared. Her eyes were red and swollen, and she was sniffling, a handkerchief clutched in one gnarled hand. She looked to be in her seventies or eighties. She smiled when she saw Sloth, but when she glanced in my direction, that smile faltered. "Sloth," she breathed. "It's nice to see you, honey. I wasn't expecting any visitors." She glanced at me again. "Who's your friend?"

Sloth put her hand on the small of my back and encouraged me forward. "Mrs. Romanowsky, this is Pride. Pride, this is Mrs. Romanowsky. We live at Sinful House together on the same TV show. I thought it would be nice to bring one of my housemates along. Is it all right?"

The woman looked me over from head to foot, evaluating me. I was glad I'd worn my good jeans and not the ones with the holes in the knees. After a moment, she gave in and stepped aside so we could enter.

The inside of her home was modest, especially for a

woman who was supposed to have money. I saw nothing ostentatious or conspicuous. Nothing stood out as extravagant. In fact, the place was downright cozy. Everything was decorated traditionally, with plush upholstery and floral paper on the walls. Still life paintings added homey accents to the living room and hallway. Upstairs, I heard the twittering of birds.

"Sun conures," she said, gesturing toward her second floor. "A gift from my son. I've never been much of a pet person myself, but strangely, I find those birds comforting. Although they do make a bit of a racket. I apologize for that."

Eleanor led us into the living room, where Sloth and I sat on a couch covered in afghans. The accompanying coffee table was dotted with doilies. Eleanor ambled toward the kitchen. "Can I get you two anything to drink? I have a kettle on for tea," she said. "I know most young people don't drink tea, though."

My enthusiasm for tea was very low. "I'm fine. I'd really just like to ask you—"

Sloth elbowed me sharply in the side and shot me a dark look. I took the none-too-subtle hint and called out, "Tea sounds lovely," just as Sloth said, "I'd love some!"

While Eleanor busied herself in a kitchen, I leaned toward Sloth and whispered, "I hate tea."

Sloth held a finger to her lips. "You don't have to drink it. But it's nice to accept hospitality when it's offered. Plus, you can't just launch into an interrogation. You *promised.*"

A moment later, Eleanor returned with a tea tray set for three. She poured our cups and dropped sugar cubes in each. I accepted mine but didn't drink, placing it on my lap. Sloth gave me an almost imperceptible smile.

"I'm sorry to hear about your son," I said. I hoped that wasn't too direct, but I really wanted to get to Walt sooner than later. "Were the two of you very close?"

Eleanor sighed and dabbed at her eyes. The teacup rattled in her hands. "Yes. Very. For most of his life, it was Walt and me against the world. Walt was an oops baby; I was 45 when he was born. His father left early on, but Walt and I were like peas and carrots. We did everything together. I was a very involved mother. It wasn't until recently that we started to drift apart. And by recently, I mean, oh, the last five or so years. That's when things started getting strange."

I tried not to look too eager when I asked, "Strange how?"

Eleanor sighed, her eyes traveling the room as though the knickknacks and tchotchkes would give her the answers I was seeking. "Walt was involved with an organization he discovered online. I don't know much about them, but…" She sighed and looked down into her tea. "Well, Walt was always a strange boy. I don't deny that. Today, they'd say he was somewhere on the spectrum, but we just called him peculiar back then and didn't overthink it. He was a loner most of his life, and as an adult, he wasn't much different. So when he met that group on the internet, I was glad for him. It gave him something to do. A social life, you know. But after a while, I admit I grew a bit jealous. He spent so much more time with them than with me."

I nodded and tried a sip of the tea. It tasted like hot

water and leaves, like all other teas. I didn't know how people drank this stuff. "He was spending time with them online?"

Eleanor's eyes grew wide as she shook her head. "Oh, no. He met up with them in real life. Days at a time, sometimes. At first, it was just a day or two. But as time went on, his trips got longer and longer. His check-ins grew more infrequent. And to make things worse, when I *did* see him, he seemed troubled. Secretive. I didn't like the change I saw in him, not at all. I tried to ask him about it. But you know how men are. They don't like women to get involved in their private lives. Especially their mothers."

I didn't know anything about men and their mothers, but I was willing to take her word for it. "So he met this group about five years ago?"

Eleanor nodded. "That's right."

I set my tea on the table, hoping that my attempt at drinking it would be noted and appreciated, at least by Sloth. I sank back into the couch and crossed my legs, folding my hands in my lap. "Do you know *anything* about the group?"

For the first time, Eleanor looked nervous. She, too, set her teacup on the tray and began fussing with her hair, brushing stray locks behind her ears. She cleared her throat a few times and fiddled with her necklace, twining the chain around wrinkled fingers. Finally, she met my eyes. "They called themselves hunters," she said. "I found that hard to believe because my Walt had a soft spot for animals. I couldn't imagine him killing for sport. But I did find strange things in his room. A spiked collar much too big for a dog. A muzzle. And when the police found him…" She choked up, dabbing at her eyes with a handkerchief. "They said he had handcuffs in his pocket."

I glanced at Sloth to see if she was thinking what I was thinking, but Sloth was just gazing at Mrs. Romanowsky with a sorrowful expression, which wasn't helpful. So I took a chance and said, "Isn't it possible Walt was just into bondage?"

Sloth shot me a horrified look. "Pride!"

Mrs. Romanowsky looked like I'd just casually suggested she try cannibalism. "Excuse me?"

I gulped, knowing that once again, I'd stepped in it, but I couldn't turn back now, could I? "I'm just saying—"

"No, Pride, we all know what you're saying," Sloth interrupted. She gave me a look that I clearly read to mean, "Shut up right now." She turned back to our hostess. "Please, Mrs. Romanowsky. Continue."

The old woman gathered herself, angling her body toward Sloth—and away from me. "I tried to ask him questions about all this, but he wasn't saying much. He wouldn't even tell me the name of the organization. And he had a password on his computer, so I couldn't look it up myself. Believe me, I tried. I know that might make me a terrible person. But when your son is getting involved in strange activities and staying out for days without contacting you, well, you go a little crazy. You just want to keep your children safe."

Sloth reached over and took the old woman by the

hand, squeezing softly. "Nobody thinks poorly of you for trying to protect your son," she said.

I wasn't so sure about the nobody part. I would be pretty pissed if I discovered someone was snooping through my stuff for information I clearly didn't want to share, but that was beside the point, so I let it go. "Sloth mentioned you reported him missing a few times, but nobody took you seriously. Is that true?"

Eleanor's cheeks flushed hot and pink. "The Odyssey Police Department is an absolute disgrace," she spat. "When I first filed a report, they looked into it. My family comes from money, you see. And here in Odyssey, money talks. You know how it is."

I didn't, but that seemed to be the common theme over the past couple of days. "So the police helped you out because you're rich. That's what you're saying?"

She offered a matter-of-fact nod. "Yes, exactly. But after a while, all the money in the world couldn't get them to do their jobs properly. I would call and report that Walt had gone missing again, and they told me to just settle down and he'd show up eventually. Which, of course, he did. Until he didn't."

I saw the way her eyes grew liquid, and for a moment, I worried she would start crying. But it seemed she was more angry than sad. "I was fit to be tied when I heard the police referred my case to a TV network. Imagine my mortification when RealTV contacted me and asked if they could send *actors* to help me find my son." She glanced at Sloth and offered a lopsided, apologetic smile. "I didn't understand until later that you're not an actor. Which is a good thing, if you ask me. Actors are horrible people. Terrible. The only one I can remotely stand is that Charmaine Young woman, and even that is a grudging acceptance."

I frowned, pulled suddenly into my own thoughts. Why did the name Charmaine Young pique my attention? But then I remembered. She was the first victim of the fortune cookie scandal. "You know Charmaine Young?"

Eleanor shrugged one shoulder. "She was a friend of my son's—a member of a very exclusive club, if you catch my meaning. They were as different as night and day, yet thick as thieves. Charmaine has wanted to be an actress since she was a girl. Not an ounce of talent in her entire body, mind you, but that didn't stop her any. I never liked her, but I was grateful that she befriended my son. Even after all these years, they maintained their friendship. She was the first person to offer her condolences after the police announced Walt's death."

Sloth tilted her head to one side. "Is there a particular reason you don't like her, Mrs. Romanowsky?"

Eleanor heaved a sigh, her lips pressed into a thin, hard line. "My son was special, as I've said. He had a delicate mind—prone to flights of fancy. Charmaine encouraged his eccentricities. They talked frequently about the habits and habitats of supernatural beings. Leprechauns, mermaids, fairies." The older woman couldn't keep the disdain from her voice. "They took trips together—Area 51 to look for aliens. The Blue Mountains to search for Bigfoot. What kind of person does that? Who takes advantage of a delicate mind like that?"

To be honest, it didn't sound like a big deal to me. Lots of people were interested in things like aliens and pseudo-monsters; I didn't see the harm in it. I'd seen much more toxic friendships in every teen movie that came pouring out of Hollywood. But maybe there was something Eleanor wasn't telling us.

I reached for my tea, pretended to take a sip, and then placed the teacup back on the saucer. "Eleanor, would it be all right if I saw his room?"

The old woman wrinkled her chin, hands wringing at her chest. "His room? Whatever for?"

Sloth took the old woman's hand, squeezing her fingers softly. "Pride is a psychic who sometimes sees things. It might help us understand what happened to Walter."

Eleanor glanced up the stairs, still looking unsure. "Well, in that case, I suppose it won't hurt anything. It's the first room on the left. But please don't touch anything."

I left Sloth with Eleanor and headed upstairs. The door to Walt's room was slightly ajar and squeaked as I pushed it open. The room was small and neat and looked nothing like the bedroom of an adult man. It was more like a time capsule, a room forever preserved in Walt's youth.

I stepped inside, breath held in my throat. A double bed was pushed against the far wall. The bed was neatly made, and atop the pillows were a collection of stuffed animals. A roll-top desk sat in the corner, stacked with papers, books, a tablet, and a laptop. In the other corner was a bookshelf, but instead of books, it held a variety of curious items: spiked dog collars, a heavy chain, a thick leash, a metal muzzle. These must be the items Eleanor had mentioned finding.

The walls were covered in unframed paintings done in the same style as the still life paintings downstairs. These, however, were not paintings of fruits and flowers. They were of fantastic monsters: griffins, manticores, phoenixes, and others I couldn't name. I leaned in closer to examine the artwork and saw that each had been simply signed, "Walt."

On the next wall, the paintings changed. These featured cryptids: Bigfoot, the Chupacabra, the Loch Ness monster. Underneath the Bigfoot and Chupacabra paintings were plane ticket stubs—undoubtedly from the trips he'd taken with Charmaine.

On the last wall, the paintings were of regular animals—foxes, raccoons, and crows, mainly. But the last picture was the most elaborate. It depicted a seal on a beach with a cityscape in the background. I thought I made out the telltale, red-tile hip roof of Wights and Wongs. It must have been a still life of something Walt had seen here in Odyssey.

Underneath the seal was a single word scrawled in the same hand as Walt's signature. It read, "Charmaine."

I know I promised not to touch anything, but I guess I was a liar because I plucked the painting from the wall and slipped it into the back of my pants, hidden by the tail of my shirt.

———

I was heading back downstairs when a blood-curdling scream ripped through my eardrums, squeezing my heart up from my chest and into my throat. I shot down the stairs, but neither Sloth nor Eleanor were in the living room. I was about to look for them outside when I heard the scream again.

It was coming from upstairs.

I ran back up the stairs, throwing open doors and shouting for Sloth and Eleanor. The rooms were all empty. When I came to the last room, I threw the door open, beads of sweat popping out on my skin, my clothes sticking to my body. I was prepared for the worst—an intruder with a gun, a lunatic with a knife, an escaped wight with a wok of stir fry.

But I didn't find any of that.

This was Eleanor Romanowsky's bedroom. The room was larger than Walt's, with huge bay windows that faced the beach. A canopy bed took up the center of the room. At the foot of the bed stood a tall, black cage the same width as the bed.

Inside that enormous cage were two beautiful birds, both sporting red and orange plumage that mimicked the colors of the sky as the sun set over the Pacific.

And one of those birds was screaming its head off.

I crumbled with relief, leaning my weight into hands rested on bent knees. "Sun conures," I breathed, repeating what Eleanor had said when we'd arrived. When I finally caught my breath, I straightened up and stepped nearer to the cage for a better look.

I didn't know a sun conure from a pit bull, but I could see the appeal. They looked like miniature parrots with the same hooked, black bill and the same shining, black eyes. I'd never seen birds like this, not in real life. I tapped the cage with a finger, and both birds turned, heads cocked comically to one side.

"Polly wanna cracker?" I said, my voice pitched up an octave. "Polly wanna cracker?"

The birds continued to stare at me, blinking as though perhaps I'd lost my mind.

"Well, I guess you don't talk," I said, standing up straight and shoving my hands in my pockets. "But you sure can scream. You almost gave me a heart attack."

I turned to head back downstairs when a voice behind me said, "Did you know sun conures can live 30 years in captivity?"

I spun around and should not have been surprised to see the ghost girl peering into the cage, her nose pressed right up against the wires. Why she didn't go through, I don't know. The physics that ruled her world continued to mystify me. "What are you doing here?" I asked.

"What are *you* doing here?" she retorted. "This is that old woman's bedroom. I don't think you're supposed to be in here."

"I heard screaming," I said.

The ghost girl turned away from the cage, a knowing look in her eye. "Oh, yeah. They do that. That's why some people don't think they make great pets."

"Well, these were a gift," I said. "Eleanor got them from her son. And now he's dead."

The ghost's eyes grew wide. "He gave her the birds, and then he died?"

I shook my head. "I don't think the two events were related."

The ghost blew out a breath, wiping the back of her hand across her brow. "Phew. That's a relief."

I watched her from the corner of my eye, wondering not for the first time what she was doing in my life. How did she choose when to show up? *Did* she choose, or did something else precipitate her appearances? What was she still doing here on Earth? Why hadn't she gone on to…wherever the dead were supposed to go?

It was useless to ask her these questions, though. I'd already asked her a million times over the years. Well, maybe not a million. But enough to know she had no more answers than I did.

"I better get back downstairs," I said. I turned away from the birds, still watching the ghost from the corner of my eye when something strange snagged my attention.

The cage was pulsating with a faint golden glow.

I stopped, turning to face the cage again, but when I did, the glow disappeared. I stepped toward it, eyes narrow as I examined it more closely. It was a standard, if large, birdcage—or at least, it seemed that way to me, someone who knows absolutely nothing about birdcages. It stood about five feet tall with a domed top and four wheels on the bottom. It was not ornately decorated. A small plaque in the lower corner read simply, "Chenoweth." I turned my face away from the cage until it nearly disappeared from my peripheral vision. And just as it slipped almost beyond my view, the glow reappeared.

"Strange," I said, turning back around. "Does the cage glow for you?"

The ghost shook her head. "No. Does it glow for you?"

"Only sometimes." I pulled my phone from my pocket and set it to record. "I wonder—"

"Pride! Pride? Hello?"

I ducked out of the bedroom and headed down the stairs to find Eleanor and Sloth standing in the living room. "There you are," I said, acting like I'd been looking for them. "Where'd you go?"

"Mrs. Romanowsky was showing me her garden," Sloth said. "We should get going. We're expected back at the house soon." Turning to our host, she asked, "Would it be okay if I visited you again sometime?"

Eleanor's face cracked into a smile, the sadness easing out from the creases of her skin. "I would like that very much, darling. And you're welcome to bring your friend here, too," she said, flicking kindly eyes in my direction. "It's good to have the energy of young people in the house."

I helped Eleanor gather the tea and other accouterments and carry them into the kitchen. Even Sloth helped, wiping down the counters as best she could, which wasn't very good at all. Sloth and Eleanor exchanged hugs while I offered only a handshake. Still, the older woman accepted gratefully. "You two be careful," she said. "And come see me again soon."

sixteen

. . .

We weren't actually expected at the house for another few hours. So once we were on the road, I said, "I want to talk to Charmaine Young."

Sloth raised an eyebrow. "Oh yeah? What for?"

I slipped the painting out of my pants and handed it to Sloth. When she saw it, her face blanched. "Are you kidding me? Did you steal this?"

"Yes," I said. There was no point in lying. "I had a feeling about it, Sloth. I'll return it. But I also want to ask Charmaine about it."

"Charmaine," she repeated. "Walter's friend? Why?"

"Don't you think it's weird? A painting of a seal with his friend's name on it?"

Sloth examined the painting, lip curled beneath her teeth. "Is it weird? His mom said she was his only friend. Maybe he painted this for her."

"Then why didn't he give it to her? Why was it hanging on his bedroom wall?"

Sloth raised an eyebrow. "I guess those are good questions. But is that all you came up with? I thought you investigated crimes for a living."

I frowned, ignoring the reproach in her voice. "I need to know more about Walt to understand what he was doing at the restaurant that night. I like getting to the bottom of things. In my line of work, it's important."

Sloth was chewing her hair again as she gazed out the passenger window. "I can see that. If someone I loved was murdered, I'd want answers. I'd want to know why."

"Knowing why isn't always satisfying," I told her. "In fact, it rarely is. It doesn't help the families when I tell them the murderer killed their loved one because they wanted her wallet, and slitting her throat was the best way to get it. It doesn't help when I tell them their loved one died because they were in the wrong place at the wrong time. When I investigate murders, I'm trying to get justice, yes, but mostly I want to help the person lying cold in the ground. I want to help them share their final chapter. Sometimes when I touch the cadavers, I don't see their final moments at all. Sometimes I see their favorite memories. You know how they say your life flashes before your eyes when you die? It's true, at least for some people. And when I touch them, I get to see those, too. Their most private home movies."

Sloth shuddered, her skin pimpling over with goosebumps. "I wouldn't want anyone to see what's in my head," she said. "I see what's in other people's heads all the time, and believe me, it's better not to know."

I glanced over at her. "Can you read my mind right now?"

She whipped her head around and peered at me before breaking into a grin. "I don't need to read your mind to know you wanna call Charmaine Young." She fished her phone from her pocket. "I'll find her number."

I nodded. "Call her and put it on speaker."

Sloth dialed and, a moment later, placed the phone in the dashboard phone holder. "It's ringing," she said.

"Hello?" The voice on the other end was breathy and hurried.

"Is this Charmaine Young?"

A pause. "This is she. Who's calling?"

"Um, hi. This might sound weird, but my name is… Pride." I didn't know when I would stop feeling ridiculous introducing myself this way, but it wasn't today. "I'm with a reality TV show called *Sinful House* filming here in town. I'm helping Eleanor Romanowsky find out what happened to her son, Walter Romanowsky. I understand you were a good friend of his. Do you have time this evening for an interview? I'd love to ask you some questions."

I heard a scuffle and rattling on the other end like someone was rifling through a junk drawer. Charmaine sighed heavily into the receiver. "I'm sorry, but that's *absolutely* impossible. Tonight's opening night at ORCA. We're performing *A Midsummer Night's Dream*, and I'm playing Titania." I heard the wet smacking of lips and deduced she was applying lipstick. "So, as you can see, I couldn't possibly spare a moment."

"I understand," I cooed. "Perhaps later this afternoon, then? I can even meet you after the play if that works better for you."

"I'm in the middle of getting dressed even as we speak," she said. "My hair needs time for the curls to set. I need to pick up my costume from the dry cleaner, and I like to enjoy a cocktail on my own to calm my nerves before curtain. So I'm very sorry. I would love to help you, but the timing is impossible. You know how it goes for actresses," she tittered. "The show runs until next week, so I won't have a free moment until then." She paused. "Just a moment. Did you say *reality* TV show? Are you bringing a film crew?"

I balked, unsure what she meant. "What?"

"To the interview. Will I be on television?"

I blinked hard. "Well, I don't know for sure. The producers—"

But Sloth reached over and punched me in the arm. "Just say yes," she mouthed to me.

"Yes," I stammered into the phone. "Yes, you'll be on TV. Of course. Does that mean you can meet with me after all?"

"There's a party starting at 10. VIP only," she said. "I'll leave word with my manager that I've invited you as my guest. *Do* make sure to bring the film crew."

"I won't forget," I said. "Thank you for your time. You won't regret it. I'll see you then. And good luck tonight!"

Charmaine paused on the other end. "In showbiz, we say *break a leg*."

"Okay then. Break a leg!"

The line went dead.

"You almost bit the big one!" Sloth said with a laugh. "What would you have done if I hadn't been here?"

I shrugged, a grin of my own spreading over my face. "Scuffed it, I guess. Like I said, I don't like to lie, and I'm not good at it. It's a good thing you were here to keep me straight."

"You mean to remind you to fib," Sloth said.

"Toh-may-to, toh-mah-to," I said. That was another phrase I didn't like. I don't actually know a single person who says Toh-mah-to. Maybe they say that in England. I've never left the continent, though, so I have no frame of reference. "The point is, we made a good team today."

Sloth's cheeks blushed a soft pink, and she grabbed a pigtail, stuffing the end in her mouth as usual. "Yeah, it was fun. I'm glad you came with me to see Mrs. Romanowsky."

"Speaking of that," I said, "you should come with me to the party. The camera crew is off tonight, and I'll need someone to play the part. You in?"

Sloth's smile faltered, the confidence fading from her face. "Wish I could. But I try to avoid crowds. In that situation, I'd have to work so hard to keep everyone else's thoughts out of my head that I couldn't appreciate what was happening around me. It's been forever since I've gone to see a movie, even. Netflix and me? We're like this." She held up two crossed fingers.

I nodded as I maneuvered the car back toward the house. "I guess that makes sense. I should probably invite Lust to come along, anyway. This is her case, too. Besides, I know how much she wants to win this thing."

Sloth was quiet for a moment, chewing thoughtfully on her hair. Then she said, "Am I a complete jerk for thinking she doesn't have a chance to win?"

Confused, I glanced over to my companion. Her cheeks were splotchy, and she looked like she'd just tasted something unpleasant. "Why do you say that?"

"Because this is America," Sloth said with a roll of her eyes, more than an ounce of disgust cutting through her words. "The show's about finding America's favorite sin, right? But Americans are so phony. We love sex, and we revile it at the same time. We *especially* hate women who enjoy it. And even though Lust is a perfectly sweet human being, women won't vote for her because they're jealous of her, and men won't vote for her because they can't have her. Of all the housemates, Lust is the only one I feel sorry for. When the show airs, she's gonna be the one that catches the most heat."

I frowned, though not because I disagreed with Sloth's assessment. I didn't like the idea of Lust being demonized on TV. "What about Wrath? Or Greed? Those guys are awful."

"They are," Sloth agreed. "But they're also guys. People overlook that kind of behavior from men. They'll get plenty of votes."

When we arrived back at the house, Sloth went up to her room, but I was starving. I made a beeline for the kitchen but stopped when I got to the dining room. Gluttony had both a giant plate of Chinese food and a look of rapture on his face. He was so absorbed in his meal that he didn't even sense me standing there. When I spoke, he jumped. "Gluttony? Did you get that from the fridge?"

The big man stuffed a forkful of stir fry into his mouth. "Mary and Joseph, don't sneak up on a brother like that!" he exclaimed, clutching his chest in a faux heart attack. "My cholesterol's so high, it won't take much to send me to my grave."

I pointed to the food. "Was that in the fridge?" I repeated.

"Sure was," he said, shoving in another forkful. "It's not yours, is it?"

"Not anymore," I agreed. "I never would have pegged you for the jerk who steals other people's food. I thought you *liked* cooking."

Gluttony held up a fork to punctuate his words. "I like *eating*," he said. "If I have to cook to get good food in my belly, I will. But when there's leftover Chinese and nobody around to enjoy it? I'ma go in." He took another bite, his eyes rolling to the back of his head. "Plus, this food *magically* delicious, you know what I'm sayin'? This stir fry *slaps*."

"That's what I hear," I said. "Wights and Wongs is supposed to be the best Chinese in Odyssey." My stomach growled, reminding me of my mission of finding my own lunch. "Hey, you seen Lust around today?"

Gluttony gestured toward the ceiling with a fork. "She's upstairs. She ain't in a good mood, though. Fair warning."

I glanced upward, my brow furrowed. "Why, what's wrong?"

"Beats me," Gluttony said, returning his attention to his plate. "I'm just sayin', if you gonna go up there, you best be on your guard."

I stopped into the kitchen long enough to make myself a sandwich. I went ahead and made two. History told me that even upset people could be consoled by food. I wrapped Lust's sandwich in a paper towel and headed to the second floor.

Lust's door was open. I peeked my head inside and saw her lying face down on top of her covers, still as a corpse. I knocked gently on the door frame. "Lust?"

Her voice was muffled. "Go away," she called.

I stepped into the room and padded over to the bed. "I brought you a sandwich," I said. "It's not much. Just salami and swiss." I waited for a reply. When it didn't come, I said, "Want me to leave it on your nightstand?"

"I'm not hungry," she said, turning her head away from me. I heard her sniffling. "Just go away, Pride. I want to be alone."

"Sure, I get it," I said. I set the sandwich on the nightstand. "But I need your help. I need to interview Charmaine Young tonight. And I need you to pretend to be a videographer."

Lust rolled over then, turning her face toward me. Her brow was creased in either anger or frustration—I couldn't tell which. Her mouth was twisted in a frown, her liquid eyes staring daggers in my direction. "What's your problem, Pride? I said I want to be alone."

"I know what you said," I countered. "But I also

know how bad you want to win this contest. Talking to Charmaine Young will boost our popularity. I'm sure of it."

Lust groaned. "We already lost the challenge. Sloth, Envy, and Gluttony solved their case."

"We only lost some Good Samaritan points," I said. "We can still win over the viewers. You still want that, right?" When Lust didn't answer, I took a chance and sat on the edge of the bed. I rested a hand on her arm, and images flashed before my eyes: a white man in a military uniform. A South East Asian woman in a saree. They were slow dancing, gazing into each other's eyes. Then the image changed: the same man and woman, but much older, and no longer dressed in their finery. They were sitting on a couch, crying.

I withdrew my hand and pressed it against my chest. My fingers tingled. "Who are they, Lust? The woman in the white saree and the man in the military uniform?"

She was silent for a long stretch before she opened her eyes and folded her hands atop her stomach. "You saw them when you touched me?"

"I did."

She bit down on her lip, a single tear falling from the corner of her eye. "My parents," she whispered.

I swallowed. "Are they dead?"

A short, bitter laugh croaked from Lust's throat. "No," she said. "No, Pride, they're not dead. I'm just dead to them."

I fell quiet, half wishing I'd never asked and half wondering what I should say next. Finally, I slumped forward, dropping my chin into my hand. "Do you want to talk about it?"

"Does it matter what I want? I asked you to leave, but you're still here." She uttered that same mirthless laugh, and when I didn't move, she sniffled, a slow hiss of air escaping her lips. "We had a falling out, I guess you'd call it. It happened a long time ago. I've mostly made peace with it, as much as a person can come to terms with their parents disowning them. But today's my dad's birthday. I tried to call and wish him well—"

She choked on the last of these words, fresh tears seeping from the corners of her eyes. "He pretended he didn't know who I was," she said. "Said he didn't have a daughter and hung up the phone."

It's times like these when I felt most like an orphan. I had parents growing up, of course. I was adopted as a baby by a very charming, All-American couple who loved me very much and gave me everything I wanted. But my whole life, I never felt close to them. It was nothing they did. It was me. I felt like an impostor, like a…like a changeling. And while I never had the urge to seek out my biological family—after all, they'd famously disappeared with the rest of Sam Lovelace's cursed compound—a part of me felt I would never be complete without them. So I could only imagine what it felt like to be rebuked by someone who was supposed to love you unconditionally. Parents were the only people who could love you that way, really. Everyone else's love came with terms.

"I can't help who I am," she said, her voice raspy

with grief. "And I wouldn't change even if I could. I just wish…I just wish it hadn't cost me my family."

We sat together in silence for as long as I could stand, which wasn't long. After a while, I got to my feet. "Party's at 10," I said. "We'll leave here around 9:30. I'm counting on you, Lust."

I didn't wait for a reply. I slipped out of the room and closed the door softly behind me.

seventeen

. . .

Since I had hours to kill before the party, I decided to pick up the reins to the cookie investigation once again. I found my dedicated camera guy in the kitchen, drinking straight from the milk carton while standing in front of an open fridge. When he saw me, he grimaced and wiped his mouth with his sleeve. "Sorry," he said. "Old habit."

This kind of stuff is why you can't eat over at just anyone's house.

"Get your camera," I said. "We have work to do."

The cameraman, whose name I still didn't know, set the milk back in the fridge and slammed the door. He gestured vaguely in my direction. "Where's the hot girl?"

"She's not coming," I said. "She needs some alone time."

The cameraman made a sour face. "You should bring the hot girl."

"Cameramen should be seen and not heard," I said. He seemed to get the message because he just gave a lame shrug as he retrieved his equipment and followed me out to the car.

Cameron Realty California was on some of the nicest beach-front property Odyssey had to offer. The building looked like it was made entirely of glass. Portia Cameron's office was on the top floor overlooking the beach. Her receptionist was a red-haired, perky thing who flashed a smile bearing too-white teeth when I came through the door. She glanced curiously at the camera guy, who made a "Don't look at me" motion, redirecting the woman's attention. Without a hitch, she looked at me, her smile growing even wider. "Good afternoon! How can I help you today?"

I gestured with my chin. "I'm here to see Portia Cameron."

The receptionist nodded. "And is she expecting you?"

I tilted my head to the side, bemused. "How should I know?"

The woman stared at me for a moment, her mouth agape. Then she smiled awkwardly and tried again. "Do you have an appointment?"

Ah. At least that was a question I could answer. "No. I'm not here to look at houses. I'm here on city council business."

The receptionist's shoulders sagged, and she offered me a tight smile. "I'm sorry. But Miss Cameron doesn't see constituents when she's in the office. If you have a city matter, there's a website where you can add items to the next meeting agenda. Would you like me to give you that URL?"

I shook my head and peered down the hall. I could just barely make out a glass door with the name "Portia Cameron" etched in frosted letters across the front. "Is she in? I'll just be a minute."

Without waiting for an answer, I headed toward the office door. The receptionist jumped to her feet, hurrying toward me. "I'm sorry, but you can't just go back there. It's not—"

But I had already opened the door to Portia's office. Crisp, conditioned air that smelled faintly of fresh paint blasted me in the face. As I stepped inside, a woman sitting behind a desk looked up in surprise. The receptionist ran up behind me, flustered, and blurted out, "I'm sorry, Miss Cameron. They wouldn't wait. They barged right past me."

Portia held my gaze a moment before flicking her eyes to my cameraman. Then she pulled her shoulders back and sat up straighter, glancing to her assistant. A stiff smile formed on her mouth. "It's fine, Lindsey. Thank you."

Lindsey muttered a final apology before slinking out of the office, the door clicking shut behind her. Portia was sitting forward in a leather executive chair, legs crossed at the knee, hands folded atop the desk. She was the picture of icy cold professionalism. She wore a black suit precisely tailored to her diminutive frame, and a cornflower blue silk blouse. White-blonde hair was pulled into a low ponytail. Her face was framed with blunt, perfectly straight bangs. Her lashes were long and black, her eyes ice blue, her lips painted deep red. When she smiled, there was no warmth in it. "You must be from that television show *Sinful House*," she said.

I jerked my head toward my sidekick. "Camera give it away?"

For all that her smile was frigid and unwelcoming, her voice was velvety. "Which one are you, exactly? Greed? Wrath? I know you're not Lust," she said, eying my outfit with a scornful chuckle.

"Pride," I said.

When she was done sizing me up, she relaxed. "Pride. I see. Well, it's nice to finally meet you. I worked with the network for weeks. I'm glad to see my labor finally paying off."

"You worked with the network?"

Portia smirked, her eyes glittering. "Who do you think found the property for the show? I don't just find properties for people. I find people for properties."

I sighed. "I don't know what that's supposed to mean."

"Every property is special in its way. Each house, apartment, condo—even office buildings attract a certain kind of soul. Put the wrong person in the wrong abode, and it's a disaster for everyone. But when the network contacted me about this project, I knew exactly where to put you. It was paramount that I not dump you just anywhere. We had to construct exactly the right look for America's 7 Deadly Sins. I didn't want you coming to my town and living out of some hovel. How would that make us all look? I sit on the city council." She tossed her bangs from her eyes. "I have Odyssey's reputation to uphold."

"Speaking of that," I said, taking a seat across from Portia. I was only mildly annoyed that she hadn't offered. "I've been asked to look into the fortune cookie fiasco at Wights and Wongs. I'm trying to figure out who might want to sabotage their business." I offered my own icy smile. "Some sources tell me you're a good person to talk to about that."

"What exactly do you want me to say about it?"

I shrugged. "I'd take a confession."

Now, Portia's eyes came to life as she laughed, a good-natured sound only slightly edged with something bleaker. "Do you *really* think I have time to mess around with a Chinese restaurant's fortune cookies? Really, if you're the best the network has to offer, I'm worried the poor people of Odyssey stand no chance of solving their petty crimes and mysteries."

I crossed my legs, shrugging off the insult. "I understand you proposed legislation that would put the Wongs out of business. Or at least force them to remodel or move. Something about their restaurant being an eyesore? Do you have anything to say about that?"

Portia placed her elbows on the desk. She leaned forward, resting her chin in her hands. Her nails were short and square and painted red to match her lipstick. "Do you have any idea how many Odyssey residents would love to see the Wongs go out of business? Not just because their building is hideous, which it is. Not just because their gimmick is tacky, which it is. No. That horrific building is sitting on prime real estate. That lot is worth at least twice what the Wongs paid for it. This town is booming, and our moneyed families want their piece of that pie. Leland Jordan, a long-time friend and client, tried to buy the property last year. He offered the Wongs $100,000 more than the property is worth. The Wongs wouldn't sell. And if you think Leland Jordan is the only person trying to get his hands on that property, you're wrong."

I chewed on that for a minute. From my years working with the police, I knew people were almost always motivated by two things: love (or whatever they mistook for love) and greed. If someone stood to make a wad of cash from the Wongs losing their business, that put them squarely in my crosshairs. "So, who else was interested in buying the property?"

But instead of answering my question, Portia pulled out a compact mirror and flipped it open. She raised her chin, examining her lipstick. "Help me understand. You're looking for the person behind the fortune cookie situation, right?"

I nodded. "That's right."

"And let me guess. You think someone might have financial reasons to shut down the Wongs. Is that right?"

I sensed she was going somewhere with this line of questioning. I'd seen the cops do it plenty of times. She was setting me up to knock me down, and I didn't like it. "It's a good theory," I said.

"It isn't." Portia's smile slid off her lips as she snapped her compact closed. "Look, I'll be frank with you. I don't like the restaurant. I would love to tear down that building and put up a chic swimwear boutique or a lovely tea shop. But the Wongs are small potatoes. I'm in the real estate business to make *money*. I have much bigger concerns, and frankly, if I *did* want to spend my energy on ruining that restaurant, I wouldn't do it with fortune cookies. I'd do it the old-fashioned way. With blackmail and bribes." Her smile returned, but now it had a wicked bite to it. "And that's how my clients would do it, too. What's the point of having money and power if you can't use it to get what you want?"

As much as I hated to admit it, my gut said Portia was telling the truth. A quick glance around her office made it clear what her priorities were. Framed photographs of expensive properties adorned her walls with their price tags etched into the frames in gold. All the properties were in the high millions. She also had framed photographs of herself with a senator, a business mogul, and even a previous first lady. Portia Cameron loved money and clout, and I couldn't imagine her wasting her time or reputation on fortune cookies.

And if this Leland Jordan and others of his ilk were like Portia—and experience told me they were—fortune cookies were way outside their wheelhouse.

"However." Portia leaned forward aggressively, an arrogant smirk curling over her lips. "There are *others* in this town who'd love to put the Wongs out of business for reasons that have nothing to do with money. And not that you asked for my opinion, and you certainly don't deserve it, but if I were you, I'd rule out the sharks with teeth. You're looking for the soft-hearted and tender. The predator that guiles you with its vulnerability right before it tears out your jugular." When my expression betrayed no understanding—I really had no idea what this woman was talking about—Portia huffed out a disgruntled sigh. "*Liberals.*"

I stared mutely at the woman in front of me, debating whether I'd heard her correctly. *Liberals?* I searched her expression for some amusement, some tell-tale sign she was pulling my leg. I didn't see anything. Finally, I blurted, "What are you *talking* about?"

"Liberals!" She threw up her hands in exasperation. "Progressives! Left-wing socialists! This town is bursting with them. Ethical politics is the name of the game in Odyssey. Black lives matter. Trans rights are human rights. Animals are people, too."

I gaped at her, my brain unwilling and unable to process this train of thought. "Wait, are you saying that's a *bad* thing?"

Portia looked at me like I was a moron—and to be fair, I was starting to feel that way. This whole conversation had just taken a hard left. "I'm saying it's a *motive*. The only people in Odyssey who have it in for the Wongs *and* would turn to such a ridiculous *modus operandi* are those godforsaken animal rights groups. If anyone has the time and inclination to tamper with fortune cookies, it's those people."

I didn't like how she said "those people," but I

couldn't deny my curiosity was piqued. "What do the animal rights people have against the restaurant?" I asked. But then I remembered something Linda had told me at the beginning. "The tidewater goby thing? They're endangered, right?"

Portia fluttered a hand cavalierly, her expression bordering on bored. "Oh, the conservation idiots. No, I'm not talking about them. The animal rights people. Different group. Much more robust."

"Okay. Well, what about them? What do they have against the Wongs?"

Portia chuckled. "The wights, of course."

I blinked. "The wights? I don't understand."

Portia pushed away from her desk, standing. She strode over to the window, turning her back to me and gazing out over the city. "I can see that. Outsiders don't understand Odyssey at all. The town is so much more than it looks, even from this vantage point. Take the Star of the Sea, for example. That statue is supposed to guard City Hall. But for the past several months, she's been traveling all over town, appearing in the most unexpected places. Last week she showed up in front of Tigh's Dry Cleaning. The statue even had the audacity to wear a sneer instead of the beatific smile the artist gave her."

I blinked. "You have a traveling statue in this town?"

"Well, she isn't *supposed* to travel," Portia said. "And I'm sure there's a logical explanation behind her disappearances. Kids pulling a prank is my guess. But you never can tell with Odyssey. Tell me, Pride. Do you know much about supernatural creatures?"

I stammered, scratching a temple as my brows squished together. Another sharp left in this conversation. I was going to need a map to find my way back to the reason I'd come here in the first place. "Supernatural creatures? Uh, no. I can't say that I do."

Portia shrugged, unbothered. "That's okay. Most people don't. Which is why the Odyssey animal rights group has adopted their more inclusive stance. They're not just pro animal rights. They advocate for *all* sentient nonhuman entities. Animals and supernaturals alike. Since no one else is speaking up for the wights, they've added them to their platform. They want to end the indentured servitude of wights."

On its face, the idea seemed ridiculous. But the more I mulled it over, the more reasonable it seemed. If Walt Romanowsky had some kind of pro-wight liberation agenda, it might explain what he was doing at the restaurant after closing *and* why Ping attacked him. "Was Walter Romanowsky a member of these groups?"

Portia turned to face me, her brows knit together. "Who?"

"The man who was recently *murdered?*" I couldn't keep the incredulity from my words. "Surely you remember him."

Portia tsked, pressing her red lips into a hard line. "Oh, the hunter weirdo. I couldn't say. We ran in different circles."

I grunted. I bet they did. "Did the restaurant have run-ins with the activists in the past?"

"As far as I know, just demonstrations," Portia said. "Liberals with too much time on their hands virtue signaling with picket signs. You know the drill. Of the animal rights people gunning for the Wongs, Amanda Rutherford is the most vocal. She frequently solicits signatures for petitions—and she's not particular. She's an equal opportunity thorn in our flesh. Save the whales. Free the greyhounds. Reanimate the woolly mammoths, I don't know," Portia said with a roll of her eyes.

As much as I hated to admit it, a pro-wight agenda fit the crime. With a sigh, I climbed to my feet and ran a hand through my hair. "I appreciate your time, Portia. Thanks for the tip about Amanda Rutherford. Any idea where I can find her?"

"She runs a vegan bakery right by the beach called Bake Some Waves. Now, if you'll excuse me, I really need to get back to work." She gestured toward her laptop with a flick of her hand.

I smirked at the dismissal. I was already headed for the door, but maybe people like Portia always need to feel in charge. "Sure. And if I have more questions?"

She turned her attention to her computer screen and said, "Then you can make an appointment with my assistant. Good day, Pride."

———

Just as Portia promised, I found the Bake Some Waves bakery just a block from the beach. It was a cute building with a pink-and-white striped awning and hand-painted illustrations of ocean waves on the front door. A bell tinkled overhead as I entered, alerting the proprietor to my presence. A dark-skinned woman with her hair pulled into two apple-sized afro puffs greeted me. She was dressed casually in a t-shirt and jeans with a half apron tied at her waist. Her t-shirt read, "Vegans do it batter." I was sure that was a brilliant pun, but I didn't get it.

As I stepped up to the counter, the woman wiped her hands on her apron and pointed with her elbow to a display of frosted cookies. "The almond ones are half-off today," she said. "I added too much food coloring to the royal icing. Still good. But not perfect. So can I get you something?"

I folded my arms over my chest, fingers hooked under my armpits. I leaned toward the glass case, my stomach flipping with desire. My sandwich hadn't quite quelled my appetite, and the pastries looked phenome-nal. Aside from frosted cookies, she had lemon bars, chocolate brownies, jelly rolls, hand-dipped macaroons, and an assortment of other things I couldn't even name. Everything looked scrumptious. "You've got quite a selection," I said. "I think I'll try a lemon bar."

The woman grinned. "You wanna try it, or you wanna buy it? I don't do samples."

"I'll take three," I said, thinking both Lust and Sloth would happily accept an offering of sugar. The woman selected the three largest from the case and put them in a bag, which she handed to me. "Anything else?"

"Yes," I said. "I'm looking for Amanda Rutherford."

The woman pressed a hand to her chest, her smile flickering almost imperceptibly. "I'm Amanda. And you are…?"

I gestured to my cameraman as I pulled a lemon bar

from the bag. "I'm from a TV show that's filming in town. *Sinful House*. Have you heard of it?"

Amanda nodded carefully, her expression growing wary. "Sure. Everybody knows about the show." She paused, wariness sliding toward suspicion. "What do you want?"

I took a bite of the lemon bar. Tart, sugared goo melted on my tongue. My toes curled. "This is delicious," I said, hand in front of my mouth as I talked and chewed. "Wow."

"Thanks," she said. "Family recipe modified to be vegan. You don't know how hard it was to get the texture right." She paused. "So, how can I help you?"

I popped the rest of the dessert into the bag. "Sorry. Well, I'm looking into the fortune cookie debacle over at Wights and Wongs. Have you heard about it?"

Amanda nodded, misgiving easing from her face. "Of course. Everybody knows about that. I feel awful for poor Eric and Linda. They've worked hard for their success. The Wongs don't come from money or anything, you know? They're just regular people. I know how hard that is," she said, glancing around her own establishment. "I had to fight tooth and nail to get this property. But I had luck on my side. My store at least matches the aesthetic the city council wants to portray. Wights and Wongs doesn't."

I nodded. "Yeah, so I've heard. In fact, I was just talking with Portia Cameron about that very thing. She said the council has nothing to do with the Wong's troubles, though." I paused, wiping my mouth free of lemon crumbs with the back of my hand. "She also mentioned you're an animal rights activist. She said you've been pretty active in your campaign against the Wongs."

Amanda sighed, and the friendliness she'd exhibited just a moment ago seeped right out of her body. "Look," she said. "It's not a secret how I feel about the use of wights at that restaurant. Those creatures are sentient beings. They should be allowed to come and go as they please, not bound to serve shrimp fried rice to every Tom, Dick, and Harry that wanders in off the street. Besides, those wights are taking jobs that should belong to real people. Odyssey already has a growing inequality problem. Imagine if instead of using slave labor to serve their noodles, the Wongs hired local workers. A good job like that could feed a family, pay the rent. You know? It's not right what they're doing. But." She held up a hand and shook her head. "That fortune cookie business? That's got nothing to do with me."

"Do you have any thoughts on who might be involved in it?"

Amanda pressed her lips together and made a motion like she was locking her mouth with a key. "My name's Paul, and this is between y'all."

I scowled. "Your name's Amanda."

Amanda snickered, hiding her smile behind her hand. "Right. I'm just saying."

I hated it when people were obtuse. Guessing games were my least favorite. "*What* are you saying?"

"I'm saying I don't know anything, and this interview needs to be over."

What little ground I had gained earlier in our conversation was quickly giving way and I hadn't learned a thing, so I decided to change tacks before Amanda threw me out on my ear. "Did you know Walter Romanowsky?"

Amanda was still a minute before her face softened and she breathed a little sigh. "I know the name. Terrible what happened to him. They found him in a freezer," she said with a shudder.

I nodded. "It is terrible. But I have a hunch the reason he was at the restaurant that night had something to do with the wights. Was he a member of any animal-rights groups you know of?"

Amanda's shudder deepened. "That guy? No. I don't mean to speak ill of the dead, but he wasn't exactly…he wasn't someone you'd *want* in your group, you know?"

"Because he was weird?"

Amanda grunted. "Weird is putting it mildly. That's not nice, but it's true."

"Can you think of any reason he would have been at the restaurant that night?"

The baker placed a hand on her hip and shifted her weight. "Look, I barely knew the guy. I don't think he was friends with the Wongs if that's what you're asking. And as far as I know, he didn't have business with the restaurant. But beyond that, who knows?"

Amanda seemed to be holding something back, but my intuition wasn't giving me any new ideas. It seemed everyone had the same thing to say about Walt. He was a weirdo and a loner who had no particular reason to be at the restaurant after hours. And yet, he'd been there. He'd *died* there. There had to be a reason for that.

Then an idea struck me. "What about the sous chef? Ping Lau?"

Amanda's brow darkened. "What about her?"

"Is she an animal rights activist?"

"I don't know," Amanda said. "I've never seen her at any of our demonstrations. Even if she were, why would she sabotage her own company? Wights and Wongs pays her bills, and a girl has to eat. Listen." Amanda's eyes softened as she gave her head a slow shake. "Don't tell anyone I said this, but in Odyssey? Activism is more like Slacktivism. We're not like PETA. We don't throw paint on people or destroy personal property. We write petitions. Sometimes we get published in the newspaper. And sometimes, *rarely*, we demonstrate. But actually *doing* anything isn't part of our MO."

I mulled all this over, trying to find my way through this information. I wasn't sure any of it helped. "What about the conservation people?"

Amanda's eyes narrowed. "What about them?"

"What can you tell me about them?"

Amanda turned her back to me, opening the faucet and wetting a cloth. When she turned back around, her expression was murky. "I wouldn't touch those people with a ten-foot pole. Around here, you get in bed with conservationists and you make some powerful enemies. Conservationism and real estate development do not go hand in hand. And real estate is the biggest cash cow in Odyssey. You feel me?"

"I do," I said. "I appreciate your candor. Thanks for talking with me. If you think of anything, though…" I reached for a napkin and scribbled my phone number on the back. I pushed it forward, and Amanda accepted it, folding it before putting it in a pocket. "Give me a call."

"If I hear anything, I will," she said. "But don't hold your breath."

eighteen

. . .

"Is that what you're wearing?"

It was 9 p.m., and I was sitting in the living room listening to Spotify while I waited for Lust to come down. Envy appeared in front of me, plucking the earbuds from my ears.

"What are you doing?"

She gestured to my outfit. "Is that what you're wearing?" she repeated.

I looked down. I didn't know the dress code for the party, but I thought I'd chosen well. I was wearing a pair of pressed khakis, a pinstriped shirt, and my favorite suspenders. I thought I looked great, but Envy's expression said I was wrong. My cheeks burn hot with embarrassment. "What's wrong with what I'm wearing?"

Envy frowned. "Well, nothing if you're going for that Old Navy clearance rack look."

I stammered, blinking back my surprise. "I'm not," I said.

"No, I didn't think so. Look, you can't accompany

Lust to a party looking like that. She'll outshine you. I mean, she'll do that anyway, but you don't want to be *completely* mortified, do you?"

"I suppose not," I muttered.

Envy smiled, grabbing me by the wrist and pulling me to my feet. "Great. Then let's get you changed. I'm *positive* we can find something that won't make you look like Tilda Swinton's reject body double."

I didn't think I looked *that* bad, but nonetheless, I let Envy drag me up the stairs. But I drew up short when she tried to tug me into Greed's bedroom.

"Why are we going in there?" I asked.

Envy continued inside, throwing open the door to Greed's closet and rummaging around, pushing aside garments, checking out the inventory piece by piece. "You and Greed are about the same size," she said, chewing on her lips as she examined a pair of plaid trousers. "I'm pretty sure we can find you some pants in here."

I held up my hands and backed away. "Nuh uh. No way. I'm not gonna borrow Greed's pants without permission."

Envy chuckled as she rejected the plaid pants and moved on to the next pair. "What's the problem? We all live together. What's yours is mine."

I was pretty sure that wasn't how the saying went, never mind the fact that we were talking about *Greed's* things, not hers. "Come on, Envy. This is a step too far. Don't you think—"

"Aha!" Envy snatched a pair of trousers from the closet and held them up to better examine them. They were black with white pinstripes with a slight sheen in the light. She walked over and held them up to my body. "Your hips are a bit wider than Greed's, so these should hit you just above the ankle, which is *perfect!* You have very shapely ankles."

"Thanks," I said, "but I'm not wearing Greed's pants."

Envy floated out of the bedroom, stolen trousers in hand. "I think I have a blouse that will look great with these."

Still objecting to the pilfered pants, I followed Envy into her bedroom. She stalked over to the closet and began picking through her own clothes. "I *know* I brought it. It's one of my favorite blouses, and with your frame, it will just look so avant-garde."

"I don't wear *blouses*," I said, unable to keep the disdain from my voice. "Seriously, Envy, I appreciate the gesture, but——"

"Here it is." She removed the hanger from the closet and showed me the garment she'd selected. It was a bright blue oversized silk shirt—almost a tunic— patterned with white geometric line art. It clashed ridiculously with Greed's pinstripe chinos. "This is perfect."

"That is *not* perfect," I said. "I'd look like a clown. Thanks for trying, though. Honestly. I appreciate it. But no."

But Envy wasn't listening. "Let's go to your room. Can I style your hair? I love your haircut. I've toyed with cutting mine that way, too, but I don't think I have the face for it." She sighed wistfully as she reached out and ran her fingers through my hair, which I'd already styled. "Come on, Pride. Let me have some fun."

I tried objecting again, but Envy looped her arm in mine and tugged me into the hallway. However, she wasn't watching where she was going, and as soon as we tumbled into the hall, we crashed into Sloth coming up from the stairs.

I felt something cold and wet spilling down my shirt and pants. I looked down to see a dark red stain blooming through my clothes.

"Oh my God!" Sloth gasped as she bounced away from me, surveying the damage. "Oh, Pride, I'm so sorry! I wasn't watching where I was going!" She looked at the empty wine glass in her hand. "Oh, wow, I can't believe I did that."

"It's Envy's fault," I said, arms raised at my sides as the red stain continued to spread. "You couldn't have expected us."

"Your outfit's ruined," she said, staring mournfully at my midsection. "That'll never come out."

At my side, Envy smiled widely as she held up the mismatched outfit in her hands. "Thank goodness we have a spare!"

By the time I was changed into Greed's pants and Envy's blouse (we'd added leather boots and suspenders to the mix), Lust was already waiting for me in the living room.

She glanced up the stairs as I came down, her expression unreadable as she looked me up and down, taking in my outfit. "What have you done with my friend Pride?" she asked. "This is not the Pride I know."

"We had a wine accident," I said, blushing profusely. "I don't look too ridiculous, do I?"

"Not a bit," Lust said, and the look in her eyes said she wasn't kidding. In fact, her expression had gone from unreadable to *wolfish*. When she smiled at me, I felt precisely like a piece of meat.

Which, for some reason, I didn't mind at all.

"You look beautiful," I stammered.

And she did. Lust was dressed in a pair of skin-tight black and red striped pants, stilettos with razor-thin heels, and a black lace corset top. Her long, dark hair curled around her shoulders, and she'd chosen tasteful gold earrings to complement the look. Really, beautiful wasn't the right word. She looked exquisite. Breathtaking.

I was going to burst into flames if I blushed any harder. I looked away.

"We should get going," she said, glancing at the time on her phone. "We want to be fashionably late without missing all the fun."

I held up a finger. "One minute. You need a prop for tonight's ruse." I scurried off to find one of the cameramen who was done filming for the night. When I came back, I had a small video camera.

"Do you think this'll work?" I asked, showing the camera to Lust.

She smiled. "This lady's an aspiring actor, right? Yeah. I think that should work just fine." She stood up and took the camera, linking her arm in mine. With her body pressed to my side, she looked up, bright eyes twinkling. The funk she'd been in earlier was clearly gone. "Shall we?"

A frog was lodged in my throat. All I could manage was a nod.

———

The party was held at the Odyssey Regal Hotel, one of the fanciest hotels in the area. As we wended our way through the ballroom, I kept my eyes peeled for Charmaine Young. Not that I had any idea what the woman looked like. But Lust had set the video camera on her shoulder, and I was walking around smiling at everyone like a lovesick puppy. If luck was on our side at all, Charmaine Young would find us.

We had barely completed one lap around the ballroom when high, shrill laughter from the center of the floor snagged my attention. I spun on my heel to find a woman surrounded by young men, drinking prettily from a champagne flute. Unlike the other cast members who had shed their costumes for more comfortable attire, this woman was still dressed in her Titania, Queen of the Faeries costume. An elaborately curled wig strewn with glitter and flowers was topped off with a sparkling tiara. Her cheeks were painted an obscene red, and her fake lashes were so long, they hit her eyebrows. Her gown was made of sheer pink gossamer and fake leaves dotted with rhinestones to appear damp with dew.

Charmaine lifted her gaze from her admirers just long enough to catch my eyes across the room. When she saw me with Lust, and more importantly, Lust with her camera, the woman turned on a smile so bright, it burned my retinas to look directly at her. She pushed through the crowd of young men, dropping her empty glass at a nearby table as she sauntered over to us. She extended a hand to me first. "You must be Pride," she said, her words lightly accented in a manner I suspected was entirely affected. "I'm so glad to see you could make it! You didn't have any trouble getting in, did you?"

I accepted her handshake. "None at all. We were on the guest list, just like you promised. Allow me to introduce my videographer…" I turned to Lust, blind panic on my face. I had forgotten to arrange a fake name for her, and I couldn't very well introduce her as Lust or the jig would be up for sure. Luckily, Lust was quicker on her feet than I was. She stepped forward and extended her free hand. "Sita Varaprasathan," she said.

Charmaine slowly accepted Lust's handshake as she mouthed the syllables to the surname. I glanced away, choking down a chuckle at her consternation. "Should we get started, then?" I took Charmaine by the elbow and guided her to a quieter corner. "I don't want to keep you from your fans any longer than necessary."

The woman tossed a lock of curled, glittering hair behind one shoulder and nodded. "Excellent. So, how should we begin?"

"I understand you and Walt Romanowsky were friends. Is that right? How long did you know each other?"

Charmaine's eyes took on a faraway look. She licked her lips and sighed gloriously, her gaze neatly avoiding

Lust, who was pretending to record the conversation. However, I couldn't help but notice that she had turned her body to a slight diagonal, undoubtedly to appear slimmer on camera. A pro move if I'd ever seen one. "We grew up together. We were in the same class at school. Both of us are from Odyssey, which is unusual now. We're so overrun with transplants. Back then, Odyssey was a tiny, nothing beach town, and everyone knew each other. Walt was a bit of an outsider. He didn't have a lot of friends. He was strange, but I found him charming in his own way."

I made encouraging sounds as I nodded, trying not to appear impatient. I'd heard enough about Walt's strangeness. "Charming how?"

The woman dithered and twirled a hand in the air as though trying to summon an explanation from the ether. "Oh, I don't really know how to say it. Walt was fanciful. The daydreaming type. He was the kid that doodled all over his math tests, you know? Unicorns and mermaids and things like that. Even in high school, he was the kid you found alone in the art studio painting during lunch."

I nodded. "That's right. He was an artist."

Charmaine pressed her lips together. "Yes. Water-color paintings, mostly. It was an easy escape for him. A place for him to explore his imagination."

"I see. Mrs. Romanowsky says the two of you went on cryptid hunting trips together."

"Guilty as charged," she said. "My uncle was into cryptids. He passed away recently, God bless his soul. No one knew he was ill except—" She stopped short, then shook herself as though pushing away the sad memory. "Growing up, that was something my uncle and I did together. We were very close, right until the end. I was the only person in the family that shared his cryptid fascination. So when Walt suggested we go find a Chupacabra or the Jersey devil, I was game. It was fun. And it reminded me of my uncle."

"Did you ever find anything?"

Charmaine gave me a withering look. "Well, no. They're not real, you see."

I chuckled, chagrined. "No, of course not. Right. Well, can I ask you about this?" Lust retrieved the painting of the seal from her bag and handed it to Charmaine. "Have you seen it before?"

Charmaine took the painting, her fingers tracing over the seal at its center. "It's a portrait of me," she said, her voice soft.

My brows shot high in surprise. "A portrait?"

Suddenly, the cheerful facade that Charmaine had worn for us slipped from her features. She rolled her eyes, her cheeks puffing out in irritation. "All that supernatural business got *way* out of hand," she said. "It started off as a joke, but…"

"Hang on," I interrupted. "How is this a portrait? That's a painting of a *seal*."

"I know what it is." Charmaine groaned, pressing her fingertips to her forehead. "Do you know what a selkie is?"

I blinked and shook my head. "No. What is it?"

"It's a Scottish sea creature capable of shifting into a human," the woman said matter-of-factly. "I'm told they live as seals in the ocean, and when they come ashore, they shed their seal skin and live as humans." She looked around, fingers grasping nervously at strands of hair. "What does a woman have to do to get a glass of champagne around here?"

"I'll find you something in a minute," I said. "You were saying? About the portrait?"

Charmaine huffed, dragging her teeth over her bottom lip. "I asked Walt to paint me one day. This is what he came up with. I thought he was joking, but he said he saw the real me. That he knew what I *really* was —a selkie living as a human. He assured me he wouldn't tell anyone. It would be our little secret. I went along with it for a while, because why not? What could it hurt? But I should have set him straight. I should have made it clear everything we did together was all in fun. It wasn't *real*. But I never said anything. And I'll take that to my grave because that's how he got involved with those online idiots that pushed him away from me. And from his mom."

Now we were getting somewhere. "His mother said something about an organization he was involved with. Are those the idiots you're talking about?"

"You can't air that I called them idiots," Charmaine said quickly. I thought I detected a jolt of fear underlying her words. "Promise me you won't air that."

"I won't," I said, drawing an X over my heart. That wasn't a lie. None of this conversation was getting aired anyway.

Momentarily appeased, she turned to look over her shoulder, checking for eavesdroppers. When she found none, she heaved a sigh and continued. "A couple years ago, Walt got involved with this group. I don't know a lot about them except that they called themselves bounty hunters." Even beneath the electric red of her rouge, I saw a blush rise in Charmaine's face. "And not just any bounty hunters. They supposedly hunted supernatural creatures."

"Supernatural creatures?" I paused. "Like wights?"

Charmaine hesitated, then dropped her chin to her chest. "Sure. Wights, selkies, you name it."

With that simple revelation, things finally started to make sense. If Walt were a supernatural bounty hunter, it explained the secrecy, the camo outfit, and what he'd been doing at Wights and Wongs that night.

Walt hadn't been trying to *free* the wights. He'd been trying to *capture* them.

Aloud, I said, "How on Earth do you capture a wight?"

Charmaine blinked at me. "What's that?"

"A wight," I repeated, still thinking it all through. "If Walt went down to the restaurant to try and capture a wight for a bounty, wouldn't he have equipment with him?"

Still confused, Charmaine held out her hands, imploring. "Capture…? Well, I'm not sure, I…What kind of equipment?"

"I don't know," I admitted. "Ectoplasm detectors? EMF recorders? Night vision goggles? Assuming catching a wight is something you can actually do, you wouldn't just walk up and grab it, would you? They're non-corporeal. Your hand would go right through." I thought of the ghost girl and the many times I'd tried to touch or interact with her. My hands always slipped through as though she was nothing more than mist. "You'd need some kind of equipment, right?" I looked to Charmaine. "Did Walt have things like that?"

At my side, Lust sucked in a breath. "Yes, Pride. He *did* have equipment with him. The cat carrier they found at the scene. That had to be his—the Wongs said they'd never seen any of that stuff before."

I frowned, chewing on a lip. "That's true. And his mother said the police found handcuffs on his body. But can you handcuff a non-corporeal being, even with magic handcuffs? And what's the point of the cat carrier?"

For a moment, the three of us were quiet. Then Charmaine uttered a dry grumble, something between a mirthless chuckle and a groan. "You're not really filming this, are you?"

Lust and I exchanged looks. If I looked anything like she did, we looked like a couple of cats with canary feathers hanging from our mouths. "I guess the jig is up," I admitted as Lust dropped the video camera to her side. "The real camera crew is off tonight."

Charmaine waved her hand, the cloud that had settled over her evaporating as quickly as it had landed. "Oh, don't worry about it. I understand why you'd lie. You really had me going there for a minute," she said with a sly grin. "Devious bastards. You know, I've heard about the show. Seven sinful psychics living together? I auditioned with the casting director," she said with an important sniff. "But obviously, I wasn't a good fit, what with not being a psychic and all. Anyway, did you have any more questions about Walt? I really would like to get back to the party otherwise."

We were already moving back toward the center of the room, where Charmaine obviously felt most comfortable. I extended a hand, which the Queen of the Faeries graciously shook. "Thanks for your time. And don't worry—your secret's safe with me."

"What secret?"

I flashed my best impish grin. "Shapeshifting selkies must be hard to come by."

Charmaine gave me a puckish smile as she turned to drift away. But for a fleeting moment, I saw the twitch of a seal's long whiskers beneath her nose and caught the scent of seaweed floating on the air.

I blinked, and they were gone.

I watched Charmaine melt into the crowd, my eyes playing no other tricks on me. She was merely Titania, Queen of the Faeries, a dashing middle-aged woman pinning her hopes on a dream.

The whiskers and seaweed were just my imagination.

Right?

nineteen

. . .

"Come on, Pride." Lust had dropped the camera off in the coat room and was now tugging me by my shirt tails across the ballroom. "This is one of my favorite songs. Dance with me."

The deejay was playing something fast and fun from the 80s that I only vaguely recognized. But when we found ourselves in the middle of the dance floor, I folded my arms over my chest.

"I don't dance."

Lust rolled her eyes and put her hands on my arms, her fingers digging into my skin. "Of course you can dance," she said. "Just wiggle your hips to the beat. Come on."

I shook my head, refusing to budge. "I never said I *couldn't* dance."

Lust cocked her head to the side, still holding onto my arms. "So you just don't like to dance?"

"I like to dance," I said slowly. "Alone. In my room. Where no one else can see me."

She threw her head back, shoulders shaking at my expense. "You're so funny, Freak Show! Come on, I'm not taking no for an answer. I haven't had anyone to dance with in ages. No one's even looking at us."

Before I could object further, Lust wrapped her arms around my waist and pulled me close. Her hip bones jutted against mine as she rocked and shimmied to the music. She pressed her lips against my ear. "We're the best-looking couple here, you know," she teased. "Everybody wants to be us right now."

I wasn't going to look around to verify this, so I had to take her word for it. It was impossible to remain still as Lust wriggled her body this way and that. I hadn't had anything to drink, but being so close to Lust made me feel giddy, like bubbles were floating around in my stomach, but not in a bad way. Lust had a way of getting to me that was both thrilling and embarrassing. But at that moment, I didn't care. In a minute, I was laughing, and before I knew it, I was swaying in time with her, a stupid smile plastered over my face.

Next thing you know, we were dancing.

One dance turned into seven, and just as I was about to beg relief, a familiar voice rang out behind me. "Pride! Lust! You made it! I didn't know you were coming!"

I turned around to see Ruby Wong beaming at us, her eyes glittering with the joy of the evening. Unlike Charmaine, she'd changed out of her Hermia costume —at least, I didn't think Hermia wore zebra leggings and a t-shirt that said, 'How to Shoot Animals' with a camera icon beneath—and was carrying a plate of something bite-sized and delicious. I realized I was starving.

"Did you like the play?"

I disentangled from Lust's arms and scrunched up my nose. "*A Midsummer Night's Dream?* We didn't watch it. I can't stand Shakespeare."

Ruby's face crumpled, and her shoulders drooped, but she recovered quickly. "Oh. I thought—well, never mind, at least you're here now."

"I'd never watch a Shakespeare play on purpose," I continued. "Especially the comedies. They're not even funny, and *A Midsummer Night's Dream* is the worst of all. Othello at least tackles real issues—racism, ageism, you know. But the comedies—"

I was about to launch into an anti-Shakespeare diatribe when Lust elbowed me in the side, effectively shutting me up. She cut her eyes at me with a "What are you doing?" glare before turning to Ruby. "Sorry we missed it. But tonight's just opening night, right? The other nights aren't sold out, are they?"

Ruby's face brightened again. "I don't think so! You should come. Maybe just don't bring Pride." She said this last bit with more than a hint of disdain.

A moment later, a young man sidled up to Ruby, slipping an arm around her waist. He looked to be Ruby's age, handsome in a non-threatening way, and wore a v-neck t-shirt beneath a purple leather jacket. Black jeans and white Chucks with no socks completed the outfit. He looked ridiculous. He kissed the girl on the cheek before turning toward us. "Friends of yours?"

She nodded, her cheeks glowing pink from his attention. Oh, young love. I knew absolutely nothing about it. "They're helping my parents with the restaurant." Turning to Lust and me, she added, "This is my boyfriend, Lee Jordan. He's studying forensic accounting at university. He played Lysander tonight."

We all shook hands, and Lust gestured to Lee's jacket. "Nice duds," she said. She probably meant it, too. My housemates had much more adventuresome taste in clothing than I did.

Lee did a little flourish that was so mortifying, it gave me dizzying secondhand embarrassment. He didn't seem at all fazed. "It's faux. I'm vegan."

That's when I recognized his name. I snapped my fingers, jabbing the air for emphasis. "Aha! Lee Jordan. I know you. You were the last guy to get one of those creepy fortunes," I said. "You got that prediction about family being detained, and then the FBI raided your house. How did that all work out? Everything okay?"

Lee shrugged and ran a hand through his hair. "Yeah, it all worked out. That whole thing was wild, though, you know? Crazy. Right, Rubes?"

Ruby nodded. "Yeah, a total nightmare."

Something about him was tickling the back of my mind, however, and it wasn't his taste in clothes. It wasn't even the fortune cookie notoriety. It was something else. "Is your dad still in prison?"

Lee shifted his weight from foot to foot, gaze darting around our little group as he obsessively cleared his throat. "Uh, yeah, I guess? He's awaiting trial."

I nodded. "What did the FBI get him on, again?"

Lust laid a hand on my arm, squeezing gently. "Hey, maybe this isn't the time," she said.

Lee licked his lips, jamming his hands in his pockets. "Embezzlement," he said. "Some shady real estate stuff."

That's when it struck me. "Your dad's Leland Jordan, right?" I turned to Ruby. "His dad tried to buy your parents' restaurant, right?"

Ruby gaped as her eyes shot wide, and she turned abruptly to Lee. "I have no idea," she said, crossing her arms over her chest. "Did he?"

But instead of answering, the snappy dresser chuckled nervously and said, "Look, I don't know what my dad's up to. His business is his business." His smile faltered as Ruby's face remained impassive. He jammed a thumb over his shoulder and stepped back. "Hey, I'm gonna go hit the head. Catch you later." He flashed us all a peace sign before making his way to the john.

"I think I'm ready to head home," I said, feigning a yawn. I really was exhausted, but mostly I was just done being around people. "Lust, let's go fetch the camera."

As I dragged Lust through the crowd toward the coat check, my housemate looked over her shoulder, blowing a kiss at Ruby. "I'll make it to your play. Promise!"

If Ruby responded to that, I didn't hear it.

Ten minutes later, we were outside, an ocean breeze riffling our hair and raising goose pimples across my skin. I was fumbling with the keys, trying to get the car unlocked. Lust was standing next to me—too close, as usual—yawning hugely and stretching like a cat. "I had a great time tonight," she said. "You were a great date."

I finally got the door unlocked. "It wasn't a date," I said. "But I enjoyed it, too."

And then, before I knew what was happening, Lust grabbed me by the chin and crushed her mouth against mine. I was so surprised, I don't even know if I kissed her back. When she pulled away, she was smiling. "Now, it's a date."

I stared at her, my face burning hot, my mouth dry. Before I even gathered my wits, Lust was climbing into the back seat, eying me with that wolfish grin she'd worn earlier. "You coming?"

I stood on the street, keys in hand, staring at my housemate. Her hair was mussed from the dancing, her lipstick smudged from the impromptu kiss. She looked amazing. Ravishing, even. The network didn't cast her as Lust for nothing. But even as my libido begged me to throw caution to the wind and have some fun for once, my heart denied me, breaking into a thousand pieces. I stood there like a mute fool, conjuring up memories of Shayda. Her smell. Her laugh. Her eyes. Her everything. Even one romp with Lust could cost me a future with the woman I loved.

On the other hand, there were no cameramen around to capture this moment. If I jumped into the backseat with Lust, no one would ever have to know.

But I'd know.

I must have stood there too long because Lust's expression changed, cloudiness rising behind her eyes that disclosed something worse than disappointment.

However, at that moment, I didn't know what it was. "I thought you liked me," she said.

I swallowed hard, shaking my head, fingers clenched hard around the keys. My heart was beating a mile a minute, and not just from desire. "You promised," I whispered, my voice thready.

"Promised?" She stared a moment, her lips moving, eyes blinking quickly as her brows knit together. But then her expression changed. Her forehead went smooth, and color rose in her cheeks. She swallowed hard, a vein in her temple pulsing. "I'm not *charming* you, you ass. I'm seducing you the old-fashioned way. But you know what? Never mind." She threw me a dark look as she buckled in, angling her body away from me. "Your loss. You don't know what you're missing."

The awful part was, I was pretty sure I did. "Lust—"

"Forget it, Pride. Moment's passed. Just take me home."

I stood there a moment longer, questioning whether I was the biggest moron in the world and even deciding that I probably was. But it was too late now. I said nothing more as I climbed into the driver's seat and started the engine.

We were pulling into the driveway of Sinful House when I finally recognized the look I'd seen in Lust's eyes.

It was betrayal.

———

I got a late start the next day. I slept in longer than usual, then went for a jog on the beach before the rest of the house was awake. Although I was getting used to the constant cameras and the need to feel "on," I still jealously guarded my alone time.

Plus, I was avoiding Lust.

I wasn't sure what had prompted her advance, but I wasn't ready to deal with it. I was even less prepared to deal with my rejection of her, which I still wasn't sure was the right move. Weren't you supposed to take a rebound lover to get over a relationship? But I didn't want to get over Shayda. I wanted to get her back, even though a little voice in the back of my head was saying on repeat, *She's never coming back.*

What can I say? There were reasons I was supposed to be in therapy.

Freshly showered, I was sitting on the couch reading a murder mystery when Wrath walked into the living room. He was dressed in Hawaiian board shorts with a set of enormous headphones hung around his neck. When he saw me, he snapped his fingers multiple times in quick succession.

"I was just looking for you," he said.

I set my book aside. "Yeah? What for?"

"Man, you ask a guy for a favor, and then can't even be bothered to remember it!" He looked mildly disgusted, but then Wrath always looked mildly disgusted. "I analyzed that file you asked me about," he said. "Took me longer to get around to it than I thought, but hey, it's free, right?" He snorted at his own joke. "You wanna come see what I found? Or should we wait for the nympho?"

My face flushed at the mention of Lust. "Wait for her? What, is she not here?"

Wrath motioned for me to follow him upstairs. "She left with Sloth about an hour ago. You guys weren't supposed to be working together today, were you? Have you solved your case?"

I shook my head. "No, still haven't solved it. But maybe whatever you found on the audio will help."

Wrath rubbed his hands together in wicked glee. "I was pretty pumped when I found it, man. Not that it was hard, though. Beginner stuff. We're not dealing with pros here."

I'd never been in Wrath's room before, so I was utterly unprepared for what awaited me. Stepping inside was like walking into one of those 90s-era hacker movies. Aside from the tiny twin bed shoved into a corner, Wrath's room consisted entirely of monitors, computers, gaming consoles, speakers, sound mixing boards, even a turntable. The room was dark, illuminated primarily with purple and blue neon lights that glowed behind his multiple monitors. It was also hot due to the heat output from all the electronics, and the ever-present whir of computer fans provided a semi-private background for our conversation.

Wrath pulled out his gaming chair and slid into it. "Computer, turn on." The monitor came to life, and an interface for audio software glimmered onto the screen. Wrath pointed to it.

"Okay, so this is the file you gave me. By the way— where did you even get that? Who uses CDs anymore? I had to order a drive from eBay to even read the file.

That's why it took so long." He didn't wait for me to reply. "Anyway, you see this waveform here?" He pointed to a dense, wavy line. "That's the original audio track—chains rattling, ghosts moaning, organ music, stuff like that. Really amateur stuff, seriously. All the testosterone tried to leave my body each time I listened to this trash."

I thought Wrath had plenty of testosterone to spare, but I kept my mouth shut.

He pointed to the second waveform beneath the first. "This was embedded within your original audio. Separating audio tracks like this isn't easy, especially since the second track was designed to not be heard by the naked ear. But I was able to differentiate between the two tracks based on background noise spikes and overall frequency."

"I'm sure this is all very impressive," I said, "but aren't you a technopath? Couldn't you just, I don't know, snap your fingers and separate the two tracks?"

Wrath gave me a sullen look. "You need to appreciate my skill, man. Computers can only do what I *tell* them, okay?" He made an exasperated sound in his throat, then continued on. "Anyway, once I separated the two tracks, I listened to the new track. It sounded like whales humping, man."

I frowned. "What does that mean?"

"It was real slow. All the words were drawn out. That's how they hid the track without anyone noticing it. Pretty cool, actually. So I had to speed up the track. And once I did…" He grinned. "Well, I'll let you hear it for yourself."

Wrath hit the space bar, and the file started to play. The beginning of the track was blank. Then a thin, reedy voice spoke. "Freedom is the only truth. Freedom is your basic right. Win your freedom at all costs. Forget the danger. Escape."

The voice faded away, and Wrath hit the space bar again, and the audio stopped. He looked up at me expectantly. "What do you think? Cool, right?"

I worried my tongue against my teeth, brow furrowed in confusion as I thought. "What's that supposed to be? Performance art? Spoken word poetry or something?"

Wrath rolled his eyes and leaned forward, tapping fervently on the monitor. "No, man, you gotta listen with better ears than that. This is liberation philosophy, man. This is abolitionist stuff. Hardcore. Close your eyes this time and listen to it again."

I shut my eyes and let my head fall slightly forward. I took a few steadying breaths, hearing only the whir of the computers. Wrath hit the space bar again, and the audio played a second time. The ghostly voice repeated the same words. "Freedom is the only truth. Freedom is your basic right. Win your freedom at all costs. Forget the danger. Escape."

A shiver ran down my spine. I hadn't recognized the voice the first time because it was distorted and artificial, probably from either the embed or the extraction. But with my eyes closed, the voice sparked a recent memory, and an image rendered in my mind's eye, plain as day.

I knew that voice.

My mouth dropped open as realization struck. I

opened my eyes. "Oh my God. That's—" I scrubbed my hands over my face, chuckling darkly to myself. "Wow, Wrath, you did it. You solved our case."

"Hell yeah, I did!" Wrath slapped his thigh with gusto. "This is for all the teachers and step-parents who said I wouldn't amount to anything." He flipped the bird at no one—or maybe everyone—in particular.

"Yeah, you saved our hide. Or at least you saved the Wongs' restaurant. I know exactly what happened with those fortune cookies. You know, Greed's not gonna like this at all. Looks like you guys are coming in last."

But Wrath barked out a laugh, shaking his head as he spun around in his chair. "We solved ours yesterday, man. You and Lust are the big losers this week. Eat my dust." He made a rude gesture and grinned maniacally. "Now, get out of my room."

I didn't need to be asked twice.

twenty

. . .

Since we'd already lost the challenge, I didn't feel any big need to rush over to the Wongs' place to tell them what I had discovered. It could wait a few hours more. It was more important that I cleared the air between Lust and me.

I wrote a note for her that said, "I'm waiting for you in my room. Please come at your earliest convenience. – Pride." I left it on her pillow.

The door to my room squeaked open a few hours later. I'd fallen asleep while waiting for her, and when she saw me bleary-eyed and only semi-conscious, she tried to ease out of the room as quietly as she'd come in. But I sat upright and beckoned for her to come back. "I'm awake," I said. "Don't go. I was hoping we could talk."

Lust shuffled into the room and perched daintily on the edge of the bed. She twiddled her thumbs in her lap, refusing to meet my gaze. "What did you want to talk about?"

I rubbed my palms over my face and pulled myself into a fully seated position. "I want to talk about the party," I said. "I hope you understand why I rejected you."

Lust looked up sharply then, her eyes narrowed. "I'm not upset that you rejected me," she said. "I'm upset that you thought I went back on my word. I promised I wouldn't charm you, and I didn't. I was just trying to get in your pants the way any regular person would. You made me feel like a jerk. *Again.* I told you I'd only give you one chance. I won't allow anyone to make me feel that way. Not anymore."

I tried to swallow but found that my throat was dry. This whole 'confessing your feelings' thing was so much harder than it looked when other people did it. "I didn't mean to make you feel bad," I said. "I just misread the situation. I didn't think that someone like you… I mean, you know…would be interested in someone like me."

"Why would I charm you if I weren't interested in you? That doesn't even make sense." Her words were sharp but edged with something else. Hurt.

"I don't know. To get something from me?"

"Of course," Lust said, her voice cool. "That's what you really think of me, even now. It couldn't be that I was just *into you,* right?"

Silence hung thick in the air between us. Lust still wasn't looking at me, and I wasn't sure that my half-assed attempt at fixing things was working. Why was it so hard for me to just say the words "I'm sorry"? That's all I needed to do. Apologize. But instead, I was making everything worse. I knew that, and yet I couldn't make myself say the thing that would get me out of it.

That, after all, was my biggest sin. Stupid, stupid pride.

Finally, Lust looked up, and her cheeks were damp with tears. "I was 22 when my parents stopped talking to me," she said. "And the worst part is, the whole thing was a giant misunderstanding. At least, that's the gracious way to look at it. It's the way I prefer to look at it. I would rather think my family misunderstood the situation so I don't have to believe they purposefully ignored the truth staring them in the face."

I said nothing, but I hoped she could read the interest in my face. I hoped she understood I cared about her story.

"My dad had this best friend. Growing up, I called him Uncle Rick. He was a friend of the family, and we did everything with him. We went camping, went to concerts, festivals, things like that. He was closer to me than some of my actual relatives. I loved him. We all did." She sighed, flipping her hair over a shoulder. "As I got older, though, I noticed Uncle Rick looking at me differently. You know what I mean when I say differently, right?"

I felt a flush creep up my neck. "I think I get the gist of it," I said. "He was noticing you the way people who like women notice you."

Lust nodded. "Exactly. Anyway, around the time I started college, Rick started coming around a lot more often. Sometimes even when Dad wasn't home. I realized pretty quickly he was coming around to see me. I thought it was flattering. A successful, older man, showing interest in me, you know? He flirted with me. Bought me gifts. We even kissed a few times. I was eighteen and insecure…but also curious. Not just about him, but also about what I could do with my abilities. So… I'm not proud of this, but when I got a little older, I charmed him. And the little gifts turned into bigger gifts. He bought me a car. I didn't think that much of it— after all, I had just graduated from college, and that's not an outrageous gift for a college grad. Not for someone like Rick, who could afford it. But my parents saw it for what it was. An older man trying to buy his way into a young woman's life. A young woman who happened to be their daughter. A daughter who, they realized to their eternal embarrassment, was a siren."

She swallowed as a fresh tear slid down her cheek. "My parents confronted me about it. Asked if I had used my charms on Rick. At first, I said I didn't. Rick's attention began long before I charmed him. But they kept insisting. *'Rick's been a friend of the family for years! He never would have behaved this way on his own! You must have done something!'* And then I started doubting myself. Like, maybe I *had* charmed him from the beginning. My parents were mortified. Embarrassed beyond belief. I kept trying to explain how it all started, but soon, even I didn't believe it. I figured I must have done it."

She was crying openly now, shoulders shaking, her voice growing thick as her throat closed up. "I thought that was the end. But my parents went on vacation, and Rick showed up at the house again. I knew I hadn't charmed him that time. But he showed up at my house and told me he was in love with me, and he wanted to run away with me." She groaned at the memory. "I was so angry, Pride. So I did the only thing I could think of."

I gulped. "What did you do?"

She shrugged. "I called his wife and told her everything." She smirked at the memory, but there was no warmth in her face, and the grin slipped quickly from her mouth. "You should've heard the names she called me. I bet you can imagine. Instead of getting upset at her husband, the man she shared a life with, the man who vowed his life to her, she took out her anger on me. And my parents? They went ballistic. They were so furious that I tried to bust up a 'perfectly good marriage' that they stopped speaking to me. My father said he didn't have a daughter, and that was the end. I've tried for years to mend the fences between us. But they don't believe me. They won't listen. And before you ask, yes, I've talked about this in therapy. But some wounds just won't heal."

We were quiet for a long time, with only Lust's sniffles punctuating the silence. After a time, I said, "Is that why you want to win, Lust? Is your wish to earn your parents' love again? Because I hate to say this, but I don't think that's a prize the network can give you."

Without saying anything further, Lust crawled into my lap and wrapped her arms around me, face buried in the crook of my neck as she sobbed in my arms. I held her tight, not saying anything. I still hated comforting people. But Dr. Xena used to say sometimes silence is golden. I hoped this was one of those times.

When the tears finally subsided, she pulled away,

wiping her nose with the back of her hand. She turned her eyes to me, and there was no longing or passion in that gaze. Just the simple desire of someone who wanted to be loved and accepted. Part of me wanted to be that person for her. Mostly, I just didn't know how.

"I'm sorry to put all that on you," she said. "I just feel like I can open up to you."

"Don't apologize," I said. "It's nice to be trusted with something intimate like that. It's awful what happened to you." I paused. "Can I ask you a very personal question?"

Her jaw clenched, and she pinched her lips, but then she relaxed and breathed, "Okay."

"That name you gave Charmaine. Sita something? Is that your real name?"

She grinned, wiping the last of the tears from her eyes. "That's my mother's maiden name," she said. "Sita Varaprasathan. I'm half Sri Lankan. I've always thought it was a beautiful name."

I waited to see if she would offer her real name, but she didn't, so I didn't press. That was part of the mystique of the show, anyway. Some mysteries weren't meant to be solved.

Lust brushed a stray lock of hair from her eyes. "Anyway, my point is this: I never use my charms on people I care about. I don't want my ability to push people away. But, I do want to find someone to love. Someone to be in a relationship with. But it's hard because once I tell people my secret, they always think I'm using it against them. Always. I don't know why. And believe me, it causes no small amount of shame and embarrassment. It's like—what, people can't just be attracted to me? It's easier to believe I manipulated their emotions than to think they just *like* me? I mean, I know I'm a lot to handle. But am I not worthy of love?"

I absolutely didn't know what to say to that, and as usual, I was quiet for too long. Finally, Lust reached up and placed a hand on my cheek, turning my face to hers. She was so close, I felt her breath on my skin. "You don't have to say anything, Pride. I appreciate your being here and listening to me."

Again, I felt the desire to say the right thing, to be the person Lust wanted me to be. Something about her made me feel warm and fuzzy, like a kid in pajamas on Christmas morning. But I wasn't sure what that meant.

Well, that wasn't entirely true. The more I thought about it, the more I knew one thing.

I wanted Lust to win this competition. Even if losing meant I didn't get Shayda back. I wanted Lust to have the chance at happiness she deserved. And I was going to do my best to help her get it.

"You know," she said, cutting into my thoughts, "when we get our new partners for the new assignments? That'll be weird. I don't think anybody else in this house can hold a candle to you. You really are a great partner, you know?"

"Speaking of that." Gently, I eased Lust out of my lap and took her by the shoulders. "I solved the case."

Lust blinked in surprise, sitting up straighter, her shoulders squaring. "You did? When? Who—"

I released her and held up a hand. "I'll tell all of you

everything at the same time," I said. "What do you say we go down and pay the Wongs a visit?"

Lust hopped to her feet, all traces of sorrow gone from her face. "Let's get this show on the road," she said. "I'll go find the camera dude."

twenty-one

. . .

It was dinnertime, but as usual, we were nearly the only people in the restaurant. We were sitting at a large table where the wights had just brought us several platters of dumplings and a heap of noodles. The food smelled delicious, but I wasn't in the mood to eat. There was a lot to say, and I wanted to get it all out in the open as quickly as possible.

Lust and I sat next to each other, across from Linda and Eric. On the third side of the table, Ruby and Lee were making goo-goo eyes at each other. My stomach flipped over when I looked at them.

When the last of the food arrived, Linda Wong ripped the wrapper off her chopsticks and viciously snapped them into two pieces. "So, on the phone, you said you had something important to tell us. It's good news, I hope?" She popped a large helping of noodles into her mouth.

I sucked in a breath. "We've solved the case," I said.

"We know who's behind the issue with the fortune cookies."

The Wongs exchanged a surprised look and then turned wide, incredulous eyes back to me. Their gaze darted between Lust and me as though they didn't know who to look to for answers. Finally, Eric blurted out, "Well? Don't keep us waiting! Who did it? Who's responsible?"

My heart was beating loudly in my ears, but I kept my calm, turning my attention to Ruby. I kept my voice low and even when I said, "Before I reveal what I found out, Ruby, is there anything you want to say to your parents?"

The girl's brow wrinkled as she looked at me and stuffed a massive helping of dumplings into her mouth. "What are you talking about?"

I sighed. "Okay. Have it your way. But don't forget, I tried to give you an out." Reluctantly, I turned my gaze back to Linda and Eric. "It was Ruby. She was behind the whole thing from the beginning."

Ruby's eyes flew wide. "Me? That's ridiculous! This is my family's business! Why would I do something like that?"

"I wondered the same thing," I said. "But then I realized people don't always act in their own best interest. Sometimes, they act in the best interest of others." I looked to my left at the wights that floated past our table. "You were trying to free the wights. You brake for dolphins. You're a vegan. And since you admire the Kimballs so much, I guess you also believe the wights are sentient. So you wanted them free."

Linda frowned, dropping her chopsticks and dabbing her mouth with a napkin. "I'm sorry," she drawled. "But I have a hard time believing our daughter would sabotage our business."

Ruby looked at her parents, her eyes wide and round with her innocence. Her body trembled. "I *wouldn't,*" she insisted. "You know I object to the wights being here, but this…this is…" She turned her gaze back to Lust and me. "How can you sit there and *lie* about me like that?"

"I took the audio from the restaurant's soundtrack to a friend who analyzed it for subliminal suggestions," I said, unfazed. I turned to face Linda Wong. "There *was* a message encoded in your soundtrack after all. At first, I was confused about what the message said. Because I *thought* the culprit was using the subliminal suggestions against your patrons. But the track said something about freedom at all costs. Escape. Strange message if it's intended for the patrons, right? But then I remembered what Portia said about the animal-rights people and how they adopted the wights into their cause. The message on the CD was never intended for the patrons. Ruby meant to implant that subliminal suggestion in the wights. She wanted them to fight for their freedom. She wanted them to escape."

"This is crazy," Ruby said. But I noted a tremble in her voice. Her facade was crumbling bit by bit.

I gave her a reproachful look. "It was *your* voice on the audio, Ruby. Do you want me to play it for everyone?"

She looked down into her plate, her shoulders

sagging. I was glad she didn't call my bluff. I had no recording to play, but she didn't know that.

Eric and Linda were staring at their daughter, their faces unreadable. Ruby continued to stare away from us, muttering to herself, but Lee was silent. *Mysteriously* silent. His gaze was in his lap, and he hadn't looked up the entire conversation.

"I'm not sure I understand," Linda admitted. "Even if Ruby tampered with our audio, what does that have to do with the fortune cookies? That's what we need to understand. Who messed with them?"

I looked at Ruby, hoping she'd take over and explain herself, but she sat still and quiet, avoiding my gaze. I sighed. "No one," I said. "The whole thing was a ruse. No one received mysterious fortunes. No one saw the future. They were all in on it with Ruby."

Eric scrubbed his chin with the back of his hand, clearly agitated. "I don't understand."

"Everyone who claimed to get a strange fortune was friends with Ruby, had a motive, and knew a secret," I said. "They used the fortune cookie fiasco to reveal those secrets. It had nothing to do with predicting the future." The Wongs continued to stare at me, so I sucked in a breath and pressed on. "The first victim was Charmaine Young, a local actress. An actress who, by all accounts, would do or say anything for her 15 minutes of fame. Turns out, she knows Ruby. They each had leading roles in *A Midsummer Night's Dream*. If I recall correctly, her fortune said something about a family member getting sick and dying, right?"

Linda nodded. "That's right. Her uncle passed away

not long afterward. It was a shock to the community. No one knew he was sick."

"Charmaine did," I said. "She and her uncle were close. I spoke with her at the ORCA party, and she admitted she knew things about him no one else did." I recalled Charmaine's face when she'd confided in me: *"My uncle was into cryptids. He passed away recently, God bless his soul. No one knew he was ill except—"*

She hadn't completed that thought, but I had enough evidence now to finish it myself. "No one knew he was ill except *me*."

I glanced over at Ruby, who was now white as a sheet, her eyes staring holes into her lap, just like Lee. "Then there was Lee Jordan." At the mention of his name, Lee momentarily looked up, bit his lip, and looked back down. "Lee's father is Leland Jordan. I heard from Portia Cameron that he tried to buy your property, didn't he?"

Linda Wong nodded. "He made several offers, in fact. Wouldn't take no for an answer."

I nodded. "Not too long after that, Lee Jordan claimed to get a fortune cookie about a family member being detained, and then the FBI raided his house." I looked over at Lee. "Lee, do you want to tell your side of the story? Or should I keep going?"

Lee looked up, his eyes twitching as he gulped and stammered. "Freeing the wights was important to me, but this was about more than just their liberation. It wasn't even about you, Ruby," he said, casting a quick look at his girlfriend, cheeks pink with emotion. "You don't know my father. He's a bastard. He'll take advantage of anyone to make a buck. When I found out he targeted the restaurant, I was pissed. I didn't want him to get his hands on this place, so I started snooping around."

Lee gulped and ran a hand through his hair. "I had suspected my father was doing illegal business for a long time, but I couldn't prove it. I don't know how to spot fraud or whatever. But I snuck into his office and downloaded some of his files. I shared them with my accounting professor, and he tipped off the FBI. After that, I had a feeling they were going to raid our house. So when Ruby asked for my help with the fake predictions, I agreed. I knew I had something I could offer. And I knew the wights needed all the help they could get."

I turned to Ruby. "That's the gist of it, right? You got your friends—actors and animal rights people—to share secrets. Things they knew were going to happen that no one else knew about. I never talked to any of the other 'victims,' but I'm guessing they all follow the same script. Do I have that right?"

Ruby was silent for a long while, and when she finally looked up, she had tears in her eyes. "I tried to talk to you and Dad about freeing the wights," Ruby said to her mother. "I told you I believed they were sentient. I told you I didn't feel good about keeping them prisoner. They're *slaves*, Mom! But nothing I said made any difference to you. So I thought maybe if you believed the wights were harming our patrons—cursing them with unlucky fortunes—" Ruby closed her eyes, squeezing out more tears. "I had to turn to the one thing

I knew you really cared about. The customers." She was crying freely now, wiping her face and sniffling as she shrank back into her chair. "I tried to talk to you. I really did. But I'm not sorry. I did what I had to do."

Linda stared at her daughter, mouth agape, methodically popping her knuckles as she mulled over the admission. "You convinced all those people to *lie* about the fortune cookies? The whole thing was fake?"

Ruby nodded dolefully. "Like Pride said, I convinced Charmaine to do it because she knew she'd be on TV. She loves the attention. Convincing Lee to do it was easy, obviously. Plus, he had a great secret to share. The others agreed for various reasons. Some of them are animal-rights advocates, just like me. Others were actors I knew from ORCA, like Charmaine. And some of them just wanted to see our business go away."

Eric, who had been mostly silent this whole time, cleared his throat and leaned forward, elbows on the table, as threatening as anyone could look seated behind a bowl of noodles. "You did serious harm to our family business, Ruby. Do you understand that? How do you expect we'll pay for college now? Where do you think the money comes from to send you to ORCA? Did you think any of that through before you conspired with our enemies to destroy us?"

I cringed at the harshness of those words, but Ruby sat up taller, thrusting out her chest and lifting her chin in defiance. "I did think about it," she said. "And I decided our financial comfort isn't as important as their basic rights. Free them. Our restaurant doesn't need a gimmick. People will support us for our food alone. Find someone who can release the wights from this contract. I *know* it can be done. If you can find someone who sells curses, you can find someone to break them. You just have to *want* to do it. You can find *anything* online," Ruby rushed to add.

Linda and Eric fell silent, staring down into their plates. After a while, Lust broke the silence with a gentle sigh. "Your daughter didn't mean to hurt you," she said, a quiver in her voice. I looked over at her and saw the emotion in her face. I knew she was thinking about her relationship with her own parents. "She was following her heart. She's learning to be her own person who cares passionately about animals—and that includes the wights. Maybe she went about it in the wrong way," Lust said, turning an admonishing glance to the teenager, "but you should be proud of her. She's coming into her own. She's figuring out her power and how to use it in the world. She's a change agent, that one. Heck, if she doesn't have a career in acting, she definitely has one in politics!"

After another drawn-out silence, Linda turned to face her daughter, her expression softer than before. "What you did was wrong, but Lust is right about one thing. You are blossoming like a flower, and we should have taken your concerns seriously. I'm sorry about that. And if it means so much to you, your father and I will find a way to release the wights." Eric opened his mouth to object, but Linda stared him down hard until he looked away, shoulders slumped in defeat. "In the future, however, I recommend you find other ways to reach people who don't listen. Wrecking their livelihood is a bit extreme." She raised an eyebrow and stared pointedly at her daughter as she said this last part. "And Lee?" Lee looked up, a hangdog look around his eyes, his Adam's apple bobbing up and down. "I don't know if your father deserved what he got, but I'm sorry your family is going through hard times. And I forgive you for your participation in all this."

Eric leaned back, folding his arms across his chest. "I still have one last question, though," he said, his brow furrowed. "Why was Walt Romanowsky in my freezer?"

Lust and I exchanged looks, unsure where to begin. "We don't have definitive answers there," I said. "But from what we can tell, it looks like Walt was a bounty hunter."

Eric stammered. "A bounty hunter?"

"Yes," I nodded. "A *supernatural* bounty hunter. Apparently, he was here to collect the wights. We don't know how and we don't know for whom. But we suspect Ping tried to protect the restaurant. So when she saw what he was up to, she hit him over the head with a frying pan and, in her panic, dragged him into the freezer."

Linda pinched the bridge of her nose, closing her eyes, her shoulders falling low. "If you figured that out on your own, it's only a matter of time before the police reach a similar conclusion."

I bit down on my lip, glancing around to make sure no one could overhear our conversation, but the restaurant was still mostly empty. "I don't think they've figured it out yet," I said. "But you're right. Unless they're profoundly inept, they'll get there eventually. You all should be prepared for that. I know how much she means to you. And this restaurant."

The Wongs' faces blanched as they digested that information. Not only were they going to lose the wights as an attraction, but they were also likely to lose Ping as their sous chef. And they still had the city council and real estate magnates after them like hawks.

It wasn't looking good for the Wongs, and I felt terrible for my part in that. But no one ever promised justice would feel good.

What can I say? Even in Odyssey, California, life's not always a beach.

twenty-two

. . .

While the Wongs, Lust, and Lee Jordan finished their food and discussed the implications of getting rid of the wights, I went outside to stretch my legs and get some fresh air. It was a pleasant afternoon. The sky was cloudless, and a gentle breeze was blowing off the Pacific Ocean. I had half a mind to take a stroll down to the beach, but I wasn't dressed for it. I hated getting sand in my tennis shoes.

Enjoying the sunlight on my skin, I ambled around to the side of the building, admiring the property for what it was. I could see why so many real estate magnates wanted to get their hands on it. It was just a short walk to the ocean, and it was conveniently located close enough to Pacific Coast Highway for easy access, but not so close that highway noise was a nuisance. As I was making my way toward the back of the property, however, something stopped me in my tracks.

I blinked, narrowing my eyes as I pondered whether sunlight was playing tricks on me. Up ahead, a shadow danced along the wall of the restaurant. I knew that shape, but my mind wouldn't grasp it. I'd lived in California beach communities most of my life, and I'd never seen the creature capable of throwing that shadow.

It was a fox. The pointy ears, sharp little snout, and elegant legs gave it away, but there was something strange about the shadow. It didn't have just one tail. I counted approximately nine, each moving independently from the others, the shadow slithering on the wall almost like a gaggle of serpents.

I was still staring at the shadow when a voice behind me said, "You see it too, don't you?"

I didn't need to turn around to know who the voice belonged to. The ghost girl sidled up beside me, her hands in her pockets, her head tilted to one side as she watched the shadow undulating with the afternoon sunlight. "Do you know what that is?"

I shook my head. "I'm guessing it's not my imagination," I said.

The ghost laughed. "Of course not, silly. If it were your imagination, I couldn't see it, too. But I can see it, all right. That's a nine-tailed fox."

I couldn't take my eyes off the shadow. "Nine-tailed fox? I've never heard of such a thing."

The ghost girl sucked her teeth and folded her arms over her chest, glowering incredulously at me. "That's because they're not animals you can find at the zoo," she said. "They're supernatural creatures. Pretty rare here in America. You mostly only find them in Japan."

I was so used to the ghost telling me random facts about wildlife that I often tuned her out. But in light of all my recent discoveries, this information was noteworthy. "A supernatural Japanese fox? What would one be doing in Odyssey, California?"

The ghost scratched her chin, thinking. "Hard to say. They like adventure and playing tricks. Most often, they shapeshift to look like humans. They especially like to be female humans. Sometimes, they try to trick rich men into marrying them. The problem is, even in their human form, they can't get rid of all of their tails. They always have at least one they can't transform." She grinned and looked up at me, her eyes wide and sparkling. "Did you know that if you put magical handcuffs on a supernatural creature, they shift back to their natural form?"

I stared at her, my mouth softly agape as my brain processed that. "Is that right?"

I was about to ask another question when the creature casting the shadow stepped into view, interrupting my thoughts.

It wasn't a nine-tailed fox, though.

It was Ping.

I glanced at the shadow and back at Ping and then to the shadow one more time. When Ping saw what I was doing, the color drained from her face, and she backed away from me, holding her hands palm out as if warding me away. "It's not what you think," she said. "It's not—I mean, I'm not—"

"I'm not going to hurt you," I said. At my words, Ping stopped moving, hands still up in the air. "I have no interest in supernatural creatures. Not even nine-tailed foxes."

She hesitated, mouth opening as she undoubtedly prepared a retort. But then she dropped her chin to her chest, her hands falling to her sides. She knew she'd been caught, and I knew I was right. Or, more accurately, the ghost was right.

Ping was a nine-tailed fox masquerading as a Chinese woman.

"Walt wasn't here for the wights," I said. I hadn't even realized I would say these words until they were already out of my mouth. All the pieces were finally falling together, and I felt stupid for not having realized it before. Of course, I didn't have all the information before. Who knew nine-tailed foxes could be running around in Odyssey, California? "Walt was looking for *you*. That's why he had the handcuffs and the cat carrier."

I glanced at the ghost, who was smiling and nodding, confirming my thoughts. "They weren't just any handcuffs," I continued. "They were *magic* handcuffs. He intended to cuff you, forcing you to shift into your true form. And then he was going to put you in the cat carrier and take you away."

Ping's hands were folded beneath her chin as her lips quivered and tears gathered in her eyes. "People like him are dangerous," she breathed, her voice strangled. "He's not good. Those people aren't good! I've heard stories. Things they do to supernaturals. Experiments. Torture. I couldn't let him take me. I'd do anything to fight for my freedom. To escape."

With these last words, her face transformed into a

snarl. And for a fleeting moment, I saw Ping as she truly was—a ferocious creature terrified for her life.

A ferocious creature who'd been bombarded with subliminal messages about escaping. About protecting her freedom at all costs. And about forgetting the danger.

I tilted my head back as I laughed toward the sky. Now, finally, everything made sense. "Ruby's subliminal message got to you. She meant to force the wights to fight for their freedom and escape. But she infected *you* with that message, too. That's why you forgot the encounter. You forgot the danger." I leaned my head to the side. "But you seem to remember now. I guess the subliminal effect wore off since the CD hasn't played since I took it."

Ping was still shaking like a leaf. Hands up to show her I meant no harm, I took a cautious step toward her. When she didn't move away, I reached down to lift the hem of her dress. Sure enough, I saw a flash of gold and red fur, the one tail she couldn't hide.

Indignant, she swatted my hand away and stepped back, cheeks glowing red with embarrassment. "That's not for you to see," she said. "Please."

I sighed and stuffed my hands into my pockets. "Listen. The police will come for you soon. They'll eventually put two and two together and determine you were responsible for Walt's death. I don't know what those supernatural bounty hunters want with you, but I *can* tell you what the police department will do with you as a human. They'll put you in jail for a long time. And just take it from me, that's not a place you want to be." I tried to smile, but it felt false, so I let it fall away with another sigh. "It's time for you to get on out of here, Ping. Change back into a fox. Get as far away from here as you can. I can't tell you what to do after that. The future is up to you. But I think your time in Odyssey is over."

Ping was still for a moment, no doubt mulling over everything I'd said. But after a while, she looked up, sad eyes down-turned, lips trembling. "Tell them goodbye for me?" she asked.

I nodded. "I will."

Without another word, the trembling woman lowered her head, and her body began to shrink, dwindling down to the size of a large house cat. Red-gold fur shot with silver sprouted from her skin. Her body was compact and strong, with liquid amber eyes that glittered with intelligence. Best of all, nine glorious tails fanned around her like a halo, catching the light from the sun.

She was miraculous.

When her transformation was complete, she posed for me, showing off her otherworldly beauty. Her mouth opened, and her tongue lolled in what I think was laughter. In the next moment, she skipped away, disappearing into the shadows where I was unlikely to ever see her again.

"Well, I guess that's that," I said to the ghost. "Your dumb facts paid off for once. Thanks for—"

But when I turned to finish my thanks, she was already gone.

twenty-three

. . .

Two weeks later, all the housemates were sitting in the living room, laughing and talking, sharing a tray of appetizers Gluttony had kindly whipped up for us. The TV was on, but nobody was watching anymore. Tensions were too high.

Today was the day. The first episode of *Sinful House* had finished airing just two hours ago. Viewers all over the country had seen us for the first time, and we were on pins and needles waiting to hear how the show was received.

"I'm so nervous, I could croak," Lust said as she dropped beside me on the couch, a fresh glass of pink champagne in her hand. "I haven't been this nervous since I took my first pregnancy test in high school."

I couldn't tell if she was joking, so I let that comment slide. "I have no doubt the public will love you," I said. "They showed all your best moments this episode. And you look amazing on camera."

Lust blushed and took a deep sip of her drink. "You're just being nice."

"No, I'm not," I countered. "I don't do that."

"That's true," Sloth said from across the room. "Pride is a no-nonsense kind of person. And I don't just know that because I can read minds."

"Get out of my head!" I snapped playfully. "You're leaving a trail of crumbs in there."

Sloth poked out her tongue. "No promises."

The front door opened, and everyone looked over to see Tricia Woodward floating through the entrance, a dazzling smile plastered on her face. As usual, she was immaculately dressed in a simple linen dress, white Keds, and hair pulled into a neat ponytail. She had a laptop tucked under her arm, and a purse slung over her shoulder.

"Hi everyone!" She pitched her voice into her trademark singsong, drifting into the living room and taking her place on an overstuffed love seat. "So, did you all watch? What did you think?"

"The editing was way unfair, man," Wrath submitted, his face twisted in a scowl. "I hardly got any screen time, man. So wrong. Plus, every scene I was in made me look like a total skeeze!"

Tricia chuckled as she crossed her legs and bounced her foot. "Maybe that's because, generally speaking, you act like a total skeeze." Her smile widened. "What about the rest of you? How do you feel about how the first assignment went?"

"I agree with Wrath," Greed said. "I definitely think our team deserved more screen time than we got. Also, the editors played up the animosity between us and the other housemates. Like that scene where Wrath called Lust a nympho? That could have been left out completely. It just made him look bad. And *me* by association."

Lust snorted, winding a lock of hair around a finger. "But he *did* call me a nympho," Lust said. "Why should that have been edited out?"

"Because it made me look bad!" Wrath shouted.

Lust sucked her teeth and smirked. "If you wanted to be portrayed in a better light, maybe you should have acted less like a twit."

Tricia held up her hands to interrupt the argument. "All right, all right. I'll take that feedback back to the editing room. Can't promise anything, though. I don't think the network will want to mess with a good thing. Preliminary numbers show our ratings were *sky high*." Tricia's eyes were large and round, glittering with the good news. "In fact, I have a feeling this may be the network's best premiere so far."

Whistles of appreciation fluttered around the room, and even I couldn't help but feel a bit chuffed by this information.

"How long do we have to wait for the official numbers?" Sloth asked. Her face was damp with nerves or excitement, and she reached for her ponytail, inching its tip toward the corner of her mouth. "I mean, I know one successful episode doesn't mean much, but I still can't stand the suspense. Am I the only one who wants to know?"

"Of course not," Envy said. "I'm so nervous I can't

even keep food down. I'm so jealous of all of you who can just snack on Gluttony's food like it's no big deal. I wish I could enjoy it."

Gluttony gestured toward the tray of finger rolls sitting on the coffee table. "Try one," he said. "I put magic in them to keep the anxiety down. Really, Envy. You ought to know better. After all this time we worked together, you still don't know how I operate?" He shook his head. "Some people just don't learn."

Envy reached for a roll and popped it in her mouth. She was still chewing when she said, "I don't feel anything."

Gluttony glowered at her. "Give it a minute, dang."

Suddenly, Tricia's phone rang. The room fell silent. Wrath snapped his fingers, and the television shut off. Tricia pressed a finger to her lips as she put the phone on speaker, setting it on her lap. "Hi, it's Tricia. You're on speaker."

The caller's voice was barely audible over the background noise on their end. It took me a minute to realize the caller was in a room full of people shouting. *Celebrating.* "Have you seen the numbers, Tricia? We did it! *Sinful House* is officially the most successful premiere the network has produced to date!"

Around the room, the housemates pressed their hands to their mouths, eyes wide. We were so quiet, you could have heard a pin drop.

"That's *amazing* news," Tricia exclaimed, making victory fists she pumped into the air. "I wish I could be there to celebrate with you guys. But I'm here at the house now. Everybody's waiting with bated breath for audience responses to start rolling in."

"I'm sending you some initial numbers and sentiment scores now," the man on the other end said. "Do you want to read them for yourself, or should I share the news with everyone at once?"

Tricia blinked in surprise, sitting up straighter. "We have comments already?"

"We do. Shall I go through the highlights?"

Tricia nodded, her hands clasped at her chest as she bit down on her lower lip. "Sure, do us the honors. We're dying here!"

The voice on the other end cleared his throat elaborately, clearly enjoying every minute of this fresh torture. "Overall, viewers identify the least with Wrath. Only 10% of audience sentiment was positive about him. Viewers liked Gluttony but say they didn't get to see enough of him to know for sure. Lust and Greed were both perceived neutrally, with very few viewers loving or hating either. Surprisingly, Sloth was well liked among all age groups, though she performed better among female viewers. Envy was also well liked, and viewers are speculating whether summoning is the extent of her abilities. And topping the charts as the most-liked housemate is Pride with a positive sentiment score of over 80%! Well done, all of you!"

Tricia hit the disconnect button on her phone. When the line went silent, the room erupted into shouting.

"Oh my God, Pride! Congratulations!"

"This is a sham, man. Last place? This is obviously Asian oppression, man. I'm being stereotyped!"

"Wow, what a ride. I wonder what'll happen next week."

"This whole thing was rigged. I want a recount."

I was sitting there like an idiot, unable to process what had just happened. It didn't mean anything. Audience sentiment mere hours after the first episode didn't mean a thing in the grand scheme of things.

And yet? It meant something to me.

Lust pulled me into a hug, lips pressed against my ear in a half whisper, half kiss. "You deserve it, Pride. Congratulations."

I disentangled myself, swallowing hard around the lump in my throat. My tongue felt huge in my mouth. "Thanks," I said. "I got lucky, I guess. They edited me well. As the show wears on, you'll pick up fans. I'm sure of it."

"Don't worry about me." She was grinning now, a twinkle in her eye. "I'm pulling out all the stops on the next assignment. We've still got a *long* way to go before any of us is crowned America's Favorite Sin!"

She slapped me on the back before standing and raising her glass in a toast. "To Pride! Freak Show outdid us all. But for the next challenge, let's show America how super sinful the rest of us can be!"

The room broke into shouts of hearty agreement. Someone shoved a glass of champagne in my face. I took a small sip and then a bigger one. Moments later, I'd downed the whole thing and was going for a second. The celebration was infectious, and before I knew it, I was laughing and taking bets on who would win the next challenge.

My money was on Lust, but who could say? Americans enjoyed all kinds of sinful pastimes.

As I downed my third glass of champagne, I was feeling good. Positive, even. Maybe coming on this stupid show wasn't the worst thing that ever happened to me, after all.

———

"Pride? Can I talk to you a moment?"

Tricia pulled me upstairs, away from the other housemates. Once in my room, she closed the door behind her. "I'd like to read you some of the viewers' comments about you. These were taken from Twitter and our Facebook page." She looked down at her phone screen and began to read. "'*Pride is my favorite housemate by far. Awkward and weird, just like me. I hope the show investigates that stuff with the commune that vanished. I'd never heard of that before.*'"

She looked at me like she wanted me to say something, but I had nothing to say to that, so I kept quiet.

Tricia continued reading.

"'*I thought I recognized Pride from that documentary about the missing artist commune! I would love to know more about that. It would be so rad if Pride looked into it. Maybe a personal challenge for the future?*'"

Tricia looked up at me, her face carefully blank. "There are dozens more like this," she said. "Viewers want to know more about what Anne Lovett found when she went up to that commune. Where those people went. What happened to them."

"There are plenty of books and documentaries about it," I said. "They can find out anything they want. All that information is available."

"It's available," Tricia agreed, "but it leads nowhere. There's no closure. No one has ever found that lost commune."

I shrugged. "Some mysteries aren't meant to be solved."

"And some are." Tricia dropped the phone to her side and took me by the elbow, leading me to the bed, where she sat on the edge. "Of all the documentaries that exist, *none* of them include you. At most, they show still photographs of your face. But none include your story. No interviews with you on the matter exist. But people want to know. What became of the baby? What does the lone survivor think happened? What's that story?"

I had a bad feeling about what Tricia wanted. I stared her right in the face. "Tell me what you're getting at, Tricia."

Her face tightened. "While you live here, the network wants you to investigate—on camera—what became of the lost commune. Where did those people go? What was really going on there? There's no one better to unearth that story than the innocent soul left behind—the baby found alone and crying who happened to grow up to become a psychic who sees ghosts."

"No."

Tricia sighed. "Don't you think they're related?

Don't you wonder if whatever happened to those people is the reason you have the talents you do?"

I folded my hands in my lap, shaking my head. "I've never thought about it."

"Don't you wonder," she pressed on, "if the child ghost that's visited you your whole life has something to do with your mysterious past?"

I stared at her, questions running through my head like wildfire. How did Tricia know about the ghost girl? None of the footage of me talking to her—or even about her—aired. "How do you—"

"I did my research before I cast you," she reminded me, her voice gentle. "I'm not an idiot. And neither are our executives or producers. They know the money shot when they see it." She licked her lips, twisting her body to face me more fully. "Let me say it this way, Pride. The network *invites* you to look into your past. It'll make for great TV. But if you don't choose to do it on your own terms, they'll find other ways to get what they want. Am I being clear?"

I chuckled, a bitter sound in the back of my throat. "Sure, Tricia. I understand. You're blackmailing me."

"It's not blackmail," she corrected. "It's *encouragement*. Look into your past, Pride. Investigate what happened to those poor people. Even if you don't find out, you'll be better off for having tried."

I knew perfectly well this conversation had nothing to do with my wellbeing, but I also knew better than to press the matter. "I'll think about it," I grunted.

"You do that," she said, standing up. "And who

knows, Pride?" She flashed me a thousand-watt smile. "Maybe you'll even thank me later."

———

As I was returning to the party, I ran into Sloth in the hallway.

"There you are," she said. "I was just looking for you." She examined my face, her head cocked to the side. "Are you okay? For someone who just won this week's vote, you sure don't look great."

"I'm fine," I lied, still thinking about Tricia's marginally veiled threat. "What's going on?"

Sloth sucked in a breath, twisting the end of her pigtail around a finger. "It's Mrs. Romanowsky. She's asked for my help—and I think I'd like *your* help."

I blinked. "Help with what?"

"After everything came out about Walter being a bounty hunter, Mrs. Romanowsky did some snooping. She hired someone to break into his laptop, and she found his emails. Apparently, Walt was in pretty deep with this group, and Mrs. Romanowsky is worried that they…well, that they're not good people."

I raised an eyebrow. They were bounty hunters capturing supernatural creatures. It was a safe bet that they weren't people you wanted to have brunch with. "Ok. And what does she want you to do?"

"She wants me to help her find out who they are and what they're doing. Why are they hunting supernaturals? And more importantly, what happens to the supes once they're caught?"

I recalled the afternoon outside Wights and Wongs when I'd confronted Ping about being a nine-tailed fox. I remembered her words clearly. She'd said, "Those people aren't good! I've heard stories. Things they do to supernaturals. Experiments. Torture."

Experiments.

Torture.

I shuddered.

"Okay," I said slowly. "Okay, yeah. I'll help you look into it. Do we have any leads at all? What did she find out?"

"Not much," Sloth said. "Just their name, really. Chenoweth International."

Something about that name tugged at a memory, but I couldn't quite place it. I was chewing on it when a voice from downstairs shouted, "Pride! Sloth! Get your butts downstairs. Tricia has an announcement!"

———

The party was well underway, and the other housemates were all inebriated when Sloth and I bounded down the steps to join the fray. "I just got the new assignments from the network," she said. "We're changing up how we do these from now on. Instead of the housemates selecting assignments randomly, producers will assign teams specific tasks. And before anyone complains," Tricia said, holding up her hand, her gaze directed pointedly at Wrath, "I'm sure they're doing it to maximize ratings, which is what we all want. After all, wish fulfillment is expensive." She said this last part with an extra gleam in her eye.

Swaying on our feet (some of us more than others—Sloth looked like she might pass out any second), we gathered around Tricia, awaiting our assignments. She looked down into her cell phone, scrolling through messages before finding the information she was looking for. "Okay, here we are. For the next challenge, the teams are as follows: Wrath, you'll be happy to know the network paired you with Pride, our audience favorite."

I felt the blood drain from my face at the thought of being stuck with Wrath for days on end. Even though I knew I'd partner with everyone eventually, I had hoped I'd get lucky and find myself with Envy or even Sloth. But though my heart was sinking with the news, Wrath was blissful—as blissful as he ever was, anyway. He was punching the air, bottom lip folded beneath his teeth. "Oh, yeah! That's what I'm talking about! We're gonna be an unstoppable team, man." Wrath pointed to me, a wicked smile spreading ear to ear. "The fan favorite with the house's smartest member? We got this in the bag."

"Continuing on," Tricia said, her voice rising only slightly, "Gluttony, you will be paired with Sloth. Envy, Lust, and Greed, you'll make up the final team."

Sloth turned to Gluttony, high-fiving him. "Working together again! We got it this time," she said.

"Your assignments have been sent to your email addresses," Tricia said. "Filming for the new challenge begins in the morning, but you're free to read your assignments now. And with that, I'm off. Good luck, everyone! And may the best Sin win!"

Wrath sidled up next to me, his phone already in hand. "Show me my next assignment," he said. His phone's screen flashed, and an email with the subject, "Wrath and Pride: Challenge #2" appeared.

Wrath might've been a pain in the neck, but his technopathy was pretty cool, I had to admit.

He clicked the email and read the assignment aloud. "Heiress Bailey Preston is concerned that her sister, Tamora, is being hoodwinked. For the past six months, Tamora has been talking to a man online who claims he loves her and wants to marry her. However, the two have never met or even video chatted. Help Bailey find out if Tamora's lover is who he says he is or if he's got other ulterior motives."

Wrath and I looked up, twin expressions of puzzlement on our faces. "Is this some kind of joke?" he said. "They want us to find a potential catfish?"

"There's already an entire reality show dedicated to this premise," I agreed. "Is this the best the network could come up with?"

Wrath's phone flashed again, this time with a second message, the subject of which read, "The catch."

Wrath clicked it.

"The challenge isn't as simple as it seems," he read. "The catch? Tamora's online lover claims to be the spirit of her dead husband trapped in a medium's body. Good luck!"

Again, Wrath and I locked eyes, our mouths hanging ajar. "A dead guy trapped in a medium's body? How are we supposed to prove or disprove something like that? We're psychics, but come on! Even we have our limits!"

I chuckled darkly, clapping my new partner drunkenly on the shoulder. "Welcome to Challenge #2, Wrath. Don't overthink it. We'll get started in the morning. And hey." I grinned like a fool as I stumbled toward the kitchen, looking for one more glass of champagne. "Good luck. With a challenge like this, we're probably gonna need it."

thanks for reading!

Sinful House Mysteries was so much fun to write, and I'm thrilled to share these adventures with you.

I'd love it if we kept in touch.

If you'd like to hear from me once a month, please sign up for my newsletter on my website.

If a newsletter isn't your jam but you'd still like to support me, please consider leaving a review. This is the easiest and best way to help other readers connect with the weird and wonderful cast at *Sinful House*.

See you soon!

about the author

Amber Fisher is the author of urban fantasy and paranormal mysteries ranging from sweet and delightful to dark and morbid. She lives in Austin, Texas, where she enjoys watching sci-fi shows, making things with her hands, baking, and playing tabletop games with her husband.

Connect with me at: amberfishermedia.com

Facebook at: facebook.com/amberfisherauthor

Twitter: @amberla

Sign up for the newsletter: bit.ly/332eurl